Remains
To Be Seen

A novel by
EDWARD H. ESSEX

Remains To Be Seen 2019 © Copyright Words In The Works LLC

ISBN: 978-0-9910364-1-7

Publisher: Words In The Works LLC

info@wordsintheworks.com

The Players

Phillip is an alcoholic and his drinking was largely responsible for the end of his marriage. But he's in recovery and doing well. He's not looking to jump straight into another relationship but the company of a good woman wouldn't go amiss.

Susan is a beautiful English woman of a certain age. She has been married to the same man for many years. Despite living a comfortable life in upscale Chester County, she feels lonely. Her distraction is her antiques shop, *Remains To Be Seen*.

James is Susan's husband. He was raised the son of a British Army officer and followed family tradition by joining the forces. He fought in Northern Ireland during the troubles of the 1970s—an experience that left him with emotional scars.

Sarah is a few years older than Susan. She was Susan's boss back in the soaring seventies in London. When Susan left for America, Sarah followed. Sarah was the object of Susan's brief foray into lesbianism, an experience neither woman got over.

Jennifer is Phillip's bisexual twin sister. She lives with a woman in Los Angeles where she works in the movie business. Phillip and Jennifer have an unusually—some might say, unnaturally—close relationship.

*An older woman knows herself well enough to be assured in who
she is, what she is, what she wants, and from whom.*

–Andy Rooney

*The Pleasure of corporal Enjoyment with an old(er) Woman is at
least equal, and frequently superior,
every Knack being by Practice capable of Improvement.*

–Benjamin Franklin

Phillip

The parking situation in Old Woodford Village on weekends was awful. It was a tiny village and there simply wasn't anywhere to add more parking spaces as the car population grew over the years. There were only a few businesses. A corner grocery store, a couple of real estate offices, a little restaurant, and a furnishing shop that always appeared to be closed. But the village also boasted the only movie theater in the area. As a result, the only legal places to park—a small blacktopped area behind the theater itself and a few roadside spaces—were always full well before the film started. It wasn't unusual to see a procession of seven or eight cars in front of the theater at showtime as frustrated drivers dropped off their passengers urging them to go ahead and buy the tickets while they circled the village in search of a parking space they knew didn't exist.

Making matters worse was Officer Todd. Woodford was far enough north of Manhattan to leave the wickedness of the big city behind and since it was populated for the most part by wealthy commuters and weekenders, it saw very little in the way of crime. This left the local policeman plenty of time to be extra vigilant in the parking offense department. And sure enough, Saturday afternoons would see him marching—was that a smirk on his face?—from one car to another, marking tires with his chalk stick and making sure no one overstayed their welcome.

Having missed not only the upcoming attractions and the commercials for the Chinese restaurant in nearby Kimpton, but the beginning of several movies as well, I became wise to this parking dilemma.

When I wanted to see an afternoon movie, I made sure I arrived at least an hour ahead of time. Armed with the *New York Times* and the *Post*, I would then have a coffee and sandwich in the little restaurant next to the theater and catch up on all the news—juicy gossip in the *Post's* case—before the movie started.

It was on one such Saturday in early November that I met Susan.

I had parked my car behind the theater as usual and was heading towards the restaurant when I saw a freshly painted sign that simply said: *Parking*. An arrow pointed to three car spaces in front of what looked like an unused garage. I thought I'd made a discovery—a new parking spot no less—until I saw that the spaces were reserved for *Remains To Be Seen* only.

Looking up above the garage, I saw a small clapboard house. I remembered it being someone's home at one time but now had been converted for the sole purpose of selling *Antique China and Silver from England* as a second elegantly lettered sign over the doorway read.

Thanks to my usual early arrival in the village there was plenty of time before the movie started.

Being from England myself—although at fifty-one, not yet an antique—I decided to take a quick look inside the shop before having lunch.

Susan

The shop had only been open a week or so when I first met Phillip. I knew immediately he was English by the way he hesitantly put his head round the door, almost as if this were my home and he needed to ask permission before coming in.

—Good afternoon, he said.

—Good afternoon. Please, come on in.

—Thanks. Is this new? The shop I mean, not the china and silver obviously.

He smiled as he said it. He had a nice smile.

—Yes, I replied. —We opened this week.

—I noticed the parking spaces first.

—They are a bit of a premium in the village, aren't they? I had to provide some otherwise I'd never get any customers.

—Yes, of course. Very clever name for an antiques shop, *Remains To Be Seen*.

—Thank you. Bit of a pun though.

—That's what we English are good at, isn't it? You are from England, aren't you?

—Yes, I am. Been here donkey's years though!

Phillip laughed at the Englishness of the expression as if he hadn't heard it for donkey's years. We introduced ourselves.

—Susan Birley.

—Phillip Brown.

And then we exchanged the usual: How long have you been in the States? What brought you here? Do you miss England? All the questions the English in America always ask each other. The chitchat went on a bit longer and then he glanced around the shop.

—May I look around?

—Of course.

He was very nice. A nice, polite Englishman.

Phillip

I didn't go back to Woodford Village for three or four weeks after that.

I had my children over the Thanksgiving holiday and then the next couple of weekends were taken up with Christmas shopping.

By the third weekend in December I was sick of fighting the crowds at the mall and decided to have that Saturday to myself. With the exception of my business partner and his family, I had bought all of my presents. I had spent a fortune on my kids. Kate was fifteen and learning guitar. Her wish list included amplifiers, guitar stands, and carrying cases—music is an expensive hobby.

William, at twelve, was still into video games and anything to do with computers. It was the first Christmas after my divorce from their mother and I wondered whether I had been subconsciously compensating by buying them so much. I didn't dwell on it.

I got up late, made coffee, and went out to pick up the newspapers from the end of my driveway. I checked the movie listings as I walked back to the house.

There was a special screening of *Jane Eyre* in Old Woodford. How very English. I decided to go to the 2:00 o'clock showing. It would give me an excuse to drop into *Remains To Be Seen*. I could chat with Susan about the film.

—Had she seen it? Was she going to see it? Shouldn't she? Being English and all?

I suddenly felt like a schoolboy. Why was I looking for an excuse to see Susan?

She was around fifty-five, fifty-six. She looked married even though she wasn't wearing a wedding ring. She had that self-assurance about her, the security of having had a long relationship with one man. Of having raised a family and now with them all grown up and living away from home, having opened a business. An interest of her own. That was probably what she was all about.

She was also very, very attractive. In that mature, sophisticated woman, kind of way.

I drove to Old Woodford listening to classical music on the local public broadcasting station. It provided a bland background for the thoughts going around in my mind. I found myself very excited at the prospect of seeing Susan. I obviously couldn't keep going in the shop without buying something. My business partner and his wife were great lovers of Colman's English Mustard—the real stuff, the hot powder you mixed with water—and I had noticed a beautiful silver mustard pot dated 1910 in the shop that would be the perfect gift for them. English mustard in a silver English mustard pot! I would wrap a tin of Colman's as well and give them that first, telling them *that* was their big gift. They liked a laugh. I parked in the theatre lot, gathered up the newspapers that had slid off the passenger seat and all over the floor of the car as I had wound my way around the country lanes on the way to the village, and hurried across the street to the shop.

I felt like I was on a first date. That mixture of excitement, a strange empty feeling in the stomach, and a slight dizziness at the prospect of seeing Susan.

—How are you today? Can I help you?

The question had come not from Susan, but a perfectly pleasant, nicely dressed woman probably just a little older than Susan.

—Oh, I was looking for a present for someone. The last time I was here I spoke to…Susan was it?

For some reason, I pretended not to remember Susan's name.

—Yes, Susan. She went back to London last night for Christmas. The woman smiled a polite smile. —To spend it with her husband's family. And then on to her home near Dublin.

—Oh, I said again. Her husband's family. My heart stupidly started beating faster, as if I had been caught doing something wrong. I tried to think of something to say that would cover up the look of disappointment on my face.

—No doubt hunting for more silver and china while she's there, I said.

—That's right, yes. You said you were looking for a present?

—Yes.

—Well, I can help you if you'd like. I'm Sarah. An old friend of Susan's. She smiled fondly as she said Susan's name. —Well, not old in the sense of being old, I've just known her a long time.

—Yes. Of course.

She laughed at her little joke. I didn't. I just wanted to leave.

The mustard pot was still on display among an eclectic collection of china and bric-a-brac on an oval table in the middle of the shop. I picked it up and paid for it.

Sarah

It was pretty obvious why Phillip had come into the shop. Susan had that effect on men.

I had had my share of men too, of course. Timothy was the last. He changed my life. Literally.

Timothy was a lot older than me. I was twenty-five at the time; he was fifty-two. Old enough to be my father as they say. This was before I got into the advertising agency side of marketing.

I was working in London for a radio station selling advertising airtime. Timothy had worked at all the agencies for years—he knew everyone in that world. But he had got fed up with all the politics and clients who were still wet behind the ears ripping his work apart. So he started his own little consulting business. He ticked over rather nicely with three or four small accounts and a couple of gigs a year working for the big boys in the main agency world. He segued from copywriting to design work, and then new product development. He was a one-man band in that he also planned media for his clients and handled the day-to-day administration of their businesses.

He was working with a client who had a salad dressing recipe—a family heirloom—when I met him. He had found a food producer who could make the recipe on a commercial scale. He named the product and designed the packaging. He wrote all the advertising. This included a campaign of very clever radio commercials. My name had been given to him by one of his ad world contacts and he called me to set up an appointment. He wanted to go over all the usual stuff. Demographics. Reach. Rates.

—I need to get some numbers as soon as possible. Could you come to my office? It's in my home. A bit out of central London though.

—That's okay, I said. —Where are you?

—Islington. On one of the streets behind the Angel pub.

I went quiet.

—I live in Camden Passage.

—Are you serious?

We were five minutes from each other.

—Well, do you want to come over early? Before you go into your office?

—That would be great. Shall I get there around nine o'clock?

—Yes. I'll have coffee on.

He gave me his address.

—I'll see you then, Timothy.

Timothy was gorgeous. *Well-preserved* is the term people tend to use, isn't it? But he really *didn't* look fifty-two. He was a big man. Not particularly tall, maybe your standard five-ten. Big in that he was stocky. Big barrel of a chest. Little bit of a gut hanging below that robust rib cage. But it all looked perfectly placed. The overall picture from neck down was rather pleasant. And then there was his face. Thin lips that often broke into a wide smile. Eyes that sparkled when he was talking. Hair that was thick and lush, parting naturally down the middle. He invented the word *charm*.

We flirted blatantly with each other. He kissed me on the cheek when I left. I couldn't stop thinking about him. What would it be like? With an older man? The cliché. All that stuff about experience. A lesson in sex.

Was it true?

When I had the radio numbers together, I called him. We arranged a second visit. Same time, same place. I found myself chatting away merrily to him. He was so easy to be with. A funny man. For some reason, I told him I was slow out of bed that morning—that it had taken me a long time to get ready.

—Well, you look beautiful. If I were twenty years younger…

He flashed a glance and let the thought drift.

I felt that old tingle downstairs.

—Timothy, forget being younger. You're gorgeous right now.

I couldn't believe I had come right out and said it. He laughed. We both did. As I stood up to leave, I reached across the table to gather up my things. I could feel my sweater riding up, exposing a band of skin. I could also feel his eyes on me. I turned toward him and tugged at the bottom of the sweater. Pulled it back down. He smiled. And I knew what that particular smile meant.

By my third visit, I was certain I was going to sleep with him. I got wet simply walking over there. I had put on a skirt this time—I wanted him to see my legs. High-ish heels. Well, okay. High heels. No stockings.

He opened the door with his usual smile. He kissed me on the cheek just as he had done the previous two times I visited.

Something took hold of me. I grabbed his face in my hands. I didn't let him turn away. Our eyes locked. I simply leaned in and kissed him. Once. Then again. Then a little bit longer. Then my arms were around his neck. His went around my waist. We lost our balance but not our contact as he pulled me into the hallway and pushed the front door shut. We fell against the wall. The kissing getting more and more intense. His body was hard up against me. And I mean hard. I could feel his cock through his trousers. I reached down and stroked it lightly. I cupped my hands under his balls. We slid down the wall and rolled onto the carpet runner. It scooted away from us until we were laying at an angle to it. Half on the carpet. Half on the polished wood floor.

—Let's go to the other room, he whispered in my ear. He steadied himself against the wall with one hand and pulled me up with the other. Walking backwards, he led me expertly into his bedroom, still kissing whatever part of my face was closest to him with each step.

He didn't need to undress me. I kicked off my shoes and reached around and unhooked my skirt. It slipped to the ground. I pulled my sweater up over my head. As it cleared my eyes, I saw that he was right in front of me. Naked. His strong body was like a fighter's. A wrestler. A statue. The clasp on my bra was at the front. I undid it. He simply mouthed *Oh* when he saw it fall away to reveal my breasts. He opened his arms and I collapsed into them. We fell onto the bed. I closed my eyes.

He turned me on my back. I bent my knees up. His hands went under my buttocks. I felt my panties being pulled down. Over my thighs. Over my knees. Over my ankles. Over my feet. Free. My legs parted. I felt his lips. Soft kisses inside my thighs. Pushing my legs further apart. Kissing my groin. And then suddenly—his tongue was on me. I let out a gasp.

That morning, Timothy made me feel things a man had never made me feel before. Or since.

Our love lasted a year. I was young and beautiful. He was old and beautiful.

We fucked. And fucked. And fucked. But then one morning, we both knew it couldn't go on.

The age difference that had worked to our advantage suddenly worked against us. He knew things about sex no man my age could give me. I gave him the innocence no woman his age could give him. This was no one-sided thing. We loved each other equally.

But there was no future. There would be no marriage, no kids, and no old age together. There was a looming expiration date on our relationship and we acknowledged it. Timothy told me about a job he had heard about from a headhunter. It was in the media department at MKT Advertising. I took it and it meant we would be unlikely to see each other again, even for business. There was no horrible breakup, but I was heart-broken. I fell into the arms of my best friend and discovered a whole different intimacy.

No man could replace Timothy and I simply never went back to a man again.

Phillip is about the age Timothy was when I met him.

Lucky Susan.

Susan

I had caught the British Airways flight that leaves JFK at seven on Friday evening and arrives early next morning in London. That particular flight was my idea so I could spend the whole day beforehand in the shop with Sarah.

Sarah was going to look after things while I was away. James, my husband, had left several days earlier urging me to leave with him then. I pointed out that I felt guilty enough as it was leaving *Remains To Be Seen* on the last big shopping weekend and really couldn't leave a whole two weeks ahead of Christmas. And although that was the main reason I didn't fly with James, I was appalled to find myself thinking that by staying, I might see Phillip again.

He had said he would drop in before Christmas.

–That would be lovely, I had said, maybe a little too familiarly given I had just met him.

But he didn't come in. And now I was flying through the night thinking about him. I was being silly, I decided, as I sipped a vodka and tonic before dinner. He was a good deal younger than me and women of my age aren't supposed to think the things I was thinking. Besides, I was very married. It felt like I had been married all my life. The children were grown up now. And that left just James and me at home. The children had been our bond and now that they were gone, I felt curiously lonely, even though James was as sweet to me as he had always been.

James was a bit of a loner himself at times. It started after his army tour in Northern Ireland. He would retreat into a shell that he called his *quiet time*. Listening to classical music alone in his study. Staring out of the window. It worried me when we were first married but he always said he was fine, just thinking. And as the years went by, I simply came to regard it as James being James.

As the vodka started working, I was already thinking about coming back to Old Woodford. Maybe I wouldn't stay in the U.K. right through the New Year. Maybe I'd come back a few days early. Maybe I was a little drunk.

I wanted to see Phillip again. There was no doubt in my mind about that.

I closed my eyes. The drone of the airplane engines and the vodka lulled me into an uncomfortable transatlantic sleep.

Phillip

Christmas came and went. As did my children. We had a good time but as always, there was the feeling that our time together was pressured. The clock started ticking down the moment the kids arrived.

Before I knew it, there was the inevitable phone call from their mother on the day I was due to take them back to her house.

—Haven't you left yet?

I resisted the urge to say, oh yes, hours ago, but knew I would be accused of saying the kind of smart-arse thing that was problematic throughout our marriage.

I wouldn't see the children now until the Easter school break.

After they left, I found myself thinking about Susan more and more.

It was now the middle of January and I was trying really hard to invent reasons to go to the shop and buy something.

It must be someone's birthday. Or anniversary. Or I could simply buy a present for myself.

And that's what I decided to do. Treat myself. I drove to Old Woodford and parked a little way down the street from *Remains To Be Seen*. I didn't want to park in the spaces at the shop in case I changed my mind about going in.

This was ridiculous.

I was acting like a kid.

Who's scared of the older woman? Eh?

I smiled to myself at the silly notion. I was just about to cross the street when a car horn tooted. I looked up and saw a Range Rover, British racing green, a woman at the wheel. The vehicle pulled into one of the parking spaces; the one reserved for *Susan*. The driver's door opened and Susan exited the vehicle as only an elegant, well-mannered lady can. She swung both legs around together, clasped at the knees. She was wearing black leather shoes, slightly rounded at the toe, with a two-inch heel. Her feet were pointing downwards. She slid forward on her seat until she was hovering over the road. A final push while steadying herself against the car doorframe propelled her to the ground. She landed as if she were weightless. Like a cat.

Susan was tall. About five-nine. There was something about her that was just right, *Je ne sais quoi*. Her body didn't come from a gym—she wouldn't be caught dead in a sweaty mass of bodies desperately seeking svelte-ness. Her body was her own. And she looked good in it. She had slender ankles that gave way to nicely shaped calves. She wasn't wearing stockings despite the cold weather. Her legs were lightly tanned, maybe she took a post-Christmas vacation somewhere. Perhaps a Caribbean stopover on the way back to New York.

A dark-grey skirt took over the story just below her knees. Her skirt wasn't exactly form-fitting but it didn't hide the shape of her long hips either. These tapered into a vase-like waist. I imagined following their perfect curves, a soft s-bend in the road, with my hands. Her white silk blouse tucked neatly into the top of her skirt. Pearl buttons led the way up to her breasts, which forced the fabric into a sensuous pull. She was wearing a lacy bra. White, but just enough of a shade darker than her blouse to give the viewer a hint of what she'd look like if she shed the blouse altogether. It was unbuttoned to that dangerous point.

Her nipples suddenly came alive, struggling at her bra. Clearly visible.

She caught me looking and modesty prevailed. She laid her left hand across her chest and splayed out her fingers, covering the open silk and responsive nipples but not quite covering them. Accidentally on purpose kind of thing.

Her neck rose out of the Hermes scarf that was protecting her shoulders. A shorter neck than you'd expect on one so tall. A simple gold chain showed me where I would one day lay soft, biting kisses. A heart-shaped face. Full lips glossed by a deep red lipstick. White, ever so slightly uneven teeth that were obviously the handiwork of some English dentist. The slight flaw in an otherwise flawless diamond. Her brown eyes were speckled with amber. Her shoulder-length blonde hair whispered silvery traces.

She reached back to grab her coat and turned to me, smiling.

–Well, good afternoon, Phillip. Just what I'm in need of. A good-looking man with big, strong arms.

She laughed. Yes, she was beautiful.

Susan

I had been thinking about him since I got back from my trip. I wanted to see him. I was tempted to call the number he had given me after he looked around the shop.

–Let me know if there is ever anything special you think I should buy, he had casually remarked.

The number was placed carefully in my diary. I had pulled it out, picked up the phone, and then put it down again about a dozen times.

I almost called him from Ireland.

I had attended a special New Year's Antiques Fair for the trade to kick off the post-Christmas stock-up.

You could find great pieces other dealers had overlooked back in October in their hurry to stock their shops for Christmas. Or sometimes these were pieces they knew wouldn't move during the holiday season. Customers tended to be a little more conservative around November when it came to shopping for silver. Knowing that the spending season was upon them. Not sure whether they should splash out on silver when there were so many other Christmas presents to buy.

I saw a pair of beautiful Georgian silver candlesticks that one of my favorite wholesalers, Rory McCabe, had offered me at an extremely good price. They were very heavy. Square corners at the base. Sharp edges.

–Now then, Mrs. Birley, you won't be finding these prices elsewhere you know. A quick kiss while your old man's not looking and I'll throw in a Thomas Hayter teaspoon as well.

–There's an offer, Rory. Would Mrs. McCabe be all right with that?

–Ah, now you've gone and spoiled the moment. Shall I wrap these?

I thought about a quick call to Phillip to see if he was interested. I'd even offer them at my buying price, just to make contact. But I got nervous for some reason. Silly really.

I bought the candlesticks anyway.

And now here we were at the shop. I'd just been to FedEx to pick up the sticks and a collection of spoons and forks from around 1816 to 1830 that I'd also bought. There was china as well. Lots of it. And lots of custom forms to deal with.

On the drive back I hatched a plan—a way to ensure Phillip would keep coming to the shop.

I would make him a present of a Regency soup ladle from Ireland that I had found. It was quite rare. Solid silver. 1824. Fiddle pattern. I'd explain the origins of the violin-shaped handle and talk about the marks and stamps as well as the connections between the families that made almost all the British and Irish flatware in the early nineteenth-century: The Eleys, Fearns, Chawners and Smiths.

I'd get him interested in my world—and then he would begin a collection, starting naturally, with my present. How very clever of me! I'd buy more Fiddle pattern silverware in lots but I would only sell a few pieces at a time to him.

That would keep him coming back. And maybe for more than the silver.

When I turned down Spring Lane to the shop I couldn't quite believe he was there, casually crossing the street. Even from a distance I could tell it was Phillip.

There's something in the way he moves, I sang to myself.

Phillip is comfortable in his body. He holds his back straight as he walks but seems completely relaxed at the same time.

He is tall but not skinny. He has presence. He has a body that I try not to think about too much. Broad at the shoulders, wide at the chest. No tapered waist for him but strong, solid hips that give way to a nice, neat bottom.

Oh, Susan. I couldn't help but help myself to an eyeful of it when he leaned over to look at the price on a clock the first time he came into the shop. He was wearing Levi's, which I was rather pleased to see were tight. Tight, and just right.

I watched his hands as he delicately lifted up the price tag on the clock. Long fingers. Nicely kept nails. He let the tag drop back down carefully and ran a hand through his hair. He has lots of it. Natural waves. Soft and shiny. He's probably fifty or so. But no sign of grey. Just lighter streaks of brown giving hints that one day, grey may come.

His eyes are the color of the North Sea. Slate blue. Swirling but not angry. They light up when he smiles. Which he does frequently; he seems a happy person. He holds me steady in his gaze when he speaks. Something so few men, or people for that matter, will do.

I hate when noses are described as aquiline. It always sounds like something out of a cheap romance novel. But that's what he has. An aquiline nose. Although his nostrils flare ever so slightly. I imagine him breathing hard. I imagine what might make him breathe hard.

Phillip

I helped Susan carry her FedEx boxes into the shop. They weren't large but they were very heavy.

—Worth their weight in silver, I remarked.

—Something like that, she replied.

I let her go ahead of me. I watched as she climbed the few steps to the front door of the shop. She moved with ease and elegance but very purposefully. She seemed to have a desire to cover as much ground as possible in the shortest space of time.

Susan stopped at the door, raised one leg to push against the doorframe to stay steady, and then balanced the parcel she was carrying on her knee. At the same time, she fished through her handbag for keys.

The action made her skirt rise up. She looked at me, looked at her exposed knee, but didn't say anything.

She didn't need to.

I seriously wondered whether this was going to be the moment already. The moment we would first make love. Making love seemed inevitable; it was just a matter of time. Or timing.

I heard heavy locks withdrawing their guard of the door. Holding her parcel up with both hands now, her leg went back to the ground.

Using her back to push the door all the way open, she gestured with her head to the inside of the shop. I heard an electronic beeping.

—Come in. Please. Just put that anywhere. Let me turn off the burglar alarm and I'll put the kettle on for some tea.

I followed her into the shop and put down the parcel I was carrying. I had a slight cramp from holding the box and tried to relax my muscles. She looked at my outstretched arms.

—I don't think you should be hugging me; I'm a married woman.

She gave me that look. The one I would learn to love. The one that said, *Hey, I'm flirting and I know it.* The one that all but said, *Fuck me.* I had to respond.

—How married?

—Very.

—That's what I thought.

—Don't sound so disappointed.

—Is that what I sound?

She ignored my question. This line of conversation was going to be on her terms. She was in charge. I kind of liked that. A strong woman.

—Are you married, Phillip?

I didn't particularly want to get into a conversation about my children's mother. But I couldn't ignore the question either.

—I was. I recently got divorced.

She looked me up and down. As if appraising me for auction. I felt the boys rumbling in my briefs at her audacity. She was turning me on and she knew it.

—Well, you shouldn't have too much trouble finding someone new, Phillip.

I loved the way she put my name at the end of her sentences.

—You're prime filet, Phillip.

I laughed out loud.

—I've never thought of myself like that.

She laughed and touched my arm lightly.

—Oh, I have. Trust me.

Susan

As I was pouring the tea, Phillip moved the boxes for me. He asked what was in them. I pointed to the one I knew contained Mr. McCabe's candlesticks.

—Open that one. But don't take anything out yet.

I handed Phillip his tea and pulled the box he had opened closer to me so I could reach into it. I removed the candlesticks and carefully unwrapped them. I held one up for him to see.

—Susan, it's beautiful! A pair?

—Yes. I knew you'd like them. I almost called you from Dublin to suggest you buy them. I decided to get them anyway.

—Tell me about them. Irish?

—No, actually they're English. Sheffield, of course. Solid silver. 1799. Stepped square bases. Sharp corners. They're heavy. The bases might be weighted, or *loaded*, as it's called.

Now that I had Phillip's full attention, I put my left forefinger and thumb around the candlestick's circular column just above the base. Grasping the whole base with my other hand, I slid my fingers ever so slowly up the full length of the column until I reached the fluted sconce. I looked up at Phillip and winked.

—Just over ten inches long. I mean, high.

—I think I know exactly what you meant…

—Do you now? I raised my eyebrows. —Back to the candlesticks, Phillip. These were made by one of the top silversmiths of the time, John Green & Company.

I handed the stick to Phillip and he examined the base carefully.

—I know what hallmarks are. But what about this coat of arms and the inscription?

—Well, interesting you should ask. The coat of arms is the Order of the Garter. A knighthood. King Edward—the third—was dancing with his cousin—Joan of Kent—when her garter accidently slipped down to her ankle. Everyone around her sniggered. In an act of Kingly chivalry, Edward took the garter and placed it on his own leg.

—A cross-dressing King…

I laughed.

—It actually became *the* most sought after knighthood. Very few people have it. Even to this day.

—And the inscription. A motto?

—Yes. *Honi soit qui mal y pense.*

—Which means?

I turned away from Phillip to get my tea. I looked back as seductively as I could.

—Evil on him who thinks evil.

—Really?

—Really.

Phillip

Susan had been very flirtatious when she showed me the candlesticks. The way she slid her hand up the column.

Like she was stroking a cock.

And the look she gave as she glanced at me. A look from under her eyelids. I didn't know it then, but it was a glimpse into the future.

She Glanced at Me.

She glanced at me,
I glimpsed the future,
But I didn't know it then.

She glanced at me,
The briefest look.
And then she glanced again.

She glanced at me,
Just one more time.
It seemed to linger on.

She glanced at me,
I glanced back.
And then her eyes were gone.

Thursday, January 17th.
Saw Susan again today. I want her.

Susan

Phillip wanted more tea. I wanted more of him.

I had been very, very naughty. I was saying things to Phillip I wouldn't dream of saying to James. Ever. I don't know why. Dangerous? Yes. Flirting? I could do that with the best of them. But I liked him. I felt unbelievably comfortable with him. And he aroused me, simple as that.

The best sex in your life comes later in life, a magazine in my doctor's office had promised. It was like I had actually been waiting for Phillip to turn up. And he's *very* romantic. He told me he writes poetry. Now let's see, what rhymes with *fuck?*

Interestingly, and despite my flirting nature, I'd never actually had an affair. Well, not with a man. There was Sarah, of course. All those years ago. During my brief lesbian experiment. We met when we were both working in the advertising business in London in the early seventies. I worked in the media department at MKT and Sarah was my boss. She had risen through the ranks and now headed the whole media department. All the girls in the department had taken me out to celebrate my forthcoming marriage to James. He and I had done things correctly. An engagement more for the sake of our families than for us, and then the etiquette of a waiting period. Just enough time to make arrangements for the *big day* as my mother called it. That would be at least a year away. Long enough for me to get all kinds of things out of my system.

The girls and I came out of Kettner's Champagne Bar way past midnight. Taittinger and Lanson Black Label champagne coming out of our ears. We'd been flirting with all the advertising guys who kept the place alive with their expense accounts.

–Now why would you go and do a silly thing like get married? asked one.

–You could just sleep with me and save your dad a lot of money, said another.

When I told them James was an officer in The Queen's Regiment, that he had completed his commission, and was now going Civvy Street, there was more laughter and leg-pulling.

–I wonder why he joined the Queen's? The question came from a lad who seemed decidedly gay himself and the others turned the teasing on him.

Despite making fun of me, the boys were a good laugh and I was really enjoying myself. I noticed that Sarah was keeping a watchful eye. Just my boss being slightly protective, I thought.

We milled around on the pavement at the corner of Dean Street saying our goodbyes. Sarah seemed to be lingering.

–Are you all right, Susan?

–I'm fine, Sarah. Thank you for this—for organizing this party for me. It was such a lovely evening.

–You're very welcome, Susan. You know you're one of my favorites.

All the girls poured themselves into cabs or just headed off with a bloke. Sarah looked around and then leaned forward to kiss me. Not a little peck. Not on the cheek. Not platonically. But on the lips. Maybe she was a little drunk. I certainly was. Because I let her do it.

I tasted her lipstick. I breathed in her perfume. My arms went around her neck. I kissed her like I was kissing a man. But she was gentle. I liked the different sensation. A lot. And then she suddenly pulled back. As if thinking she shouldn't have done it. Shouldn't have revealed her preferences to someone she worked with. Someone who worked *for* her.

—Shall we have a nightcap somewhere?

—That would be lovely, Sarah.

—The Zanzibar Club?

I looked at her and smiled.

Another advertising hangout? I was a little confused about the whole thing. Why had I let her kiss me? Why did she suddenly stop? Why was she now taking me to a public place? Had she chosen it for safety? So we didn't take the kissing any further? We would definitely know the late night media crowd there. There would be no kissing in front of them.

—That sounds good, Sarah.

—Let's walk.

She put her arm through mine. There didn't seem to be any embarrassment on her part about what we'd just done. We walked over to Covent Garden. It was the start of a close friendship. A very close friendship.

—*I met Sarah.*

I suddenly came out of my daydream, surprised to hear her name.

—Excuse me, Phillip?

—While you were in the U.K. I met Sarah just before Christmas. She said she was an old friend of yours.

—That's right. An old, and *special* friend, Phillip.

Phillip

Susan is married. The right thing to do would be to stop right now. Think about your own marriage, mate. And that's something I do often.

There are events from my marriage I remember distinctly, and things I am hard-pressed to recollect. Sometimes even conjuring up my ex-wife's face is difficult. It all seems so distant now.

The one thing I will never forget though is the last time we had sex. I say *we*. Lauren fucked me. Well and truly.

I had been unfaithful. The usual stupid one-off thing

that nearly every man has engaged in. And if they haven't, they've thought about it. And if any man tells you different, they're lying. Men are bastards.

But in all honesty, the idea of only having sex with one woman for the rest of my life was foreign to me, even as I walked down the aisle on our wedding day.

I used to commute to work in the city. On an early morning train, I saw a beautiful girl. Dark hair. Dark eyes. Pale skin. Pale lipstick. We exchanged furtive glances. I found myself making a special effort to get the same train the next day. And the day after that. Even when I didn't need to be in the office quite so early. It was like a schoolboy crush. Long story short, I asked her to lunch. Then dinner. Then I booked a hotel room.

I was drinking a lot then. And I made the bad choices you tend to make when you're knocking it back. The kind of choices that normally involve a member of the opposite sex. The booze also made me very clumsy.

Lauren found the hotel bill in my jacket pocket. Textbook stuff. The way all affairs come to light and yet another marriage crumbles.

We were officially separated but I was still living in the marital home and it was my last night there. I was moving into my own place the next day.

I had gone to bed early; I was camping out in the guest room now. Being alone there was a relief after sitting downstairs with Lauren pretending to be civil to each other in front of the kids.

I lay on my back in the dark, hands behind my head on the pillow. Reflections from passing car headlights blazed through the windows and crept across the ceiling. I heard Lauren come up the stairs, shutting off all the lights except a nightlight on the landing for the children. I heard her look in on them, I heard her go into the bathroom, and then I heard running water.

I had watched her take a bath a million times.

I could picture her now. First adjusting the temperature

of the water. Then looking in the mirror above the sink. She would reach down and pull her sweater or T-shirt up over her head and step out of her skirt or jeans. She would look into the mirror again as she unclasped her bra. She would raise her hands, spread her fingers, and gently smooth down over her beautiful breasts. Rubbing them softly. Tilting her head to look at her reflection as she massaged. Pleased to be free of her bra. Her nipples would stand to attention, obeying her own affectionate touch. And then she would bend and remove her panties. Bra and panties always matched. Black or dark blue. Sometimes white but never bright colors. She would gather up her hair and fasten it loosely on top of her head.

From the quietness of my room, I could hear the faucets being turned off. I pictured her stepping into the bath. I drifted and dozed off with that pleasant image dancing in my mind.

I couldn't have been asleep more than a few minutes. Darkness. Then light from the doorway flooded the room. Gentle footsteps. The door closed carefully. Darkness again. As my eyes adjusted, I could see the outline of Lauren standing next to the bed. A passing car headlight showed me she was wrapped in a towel. She dropped it. She was naked.

She drew the covers back. Climbed in beside me.

I felt her go down.

Under the covers.

She put her lips around my cock.

I could feel it growing with the rise and fall of her mouth.

Her tongue felt velvety on me. She worked around the very tip of my cock. Licking it sensuously. Caressing. When I was really hard, she slid back up to me. She smelled fresh. Of pink soap. She straddled me. I watched her loosen her hair. She laid down on me. Her hair brushing my shoulders. Her breasts flattening into my chest. Electricity between our skins. I can feel it even now. She put her lips momentarily on mine. Soft then firm. Abruptly, she pulled away. Sat back

35

up. And lowered herself on to my waiting erection. She helped me into her moistness. Was I dreaming? No. This was real. Up and down she went. With each stroke, taking me deeper and deeper inside her. She knew exactly how to make me come. My thighs tensed up, almost like I was going to get a painful cramp, but this was pleasurable. I came. Dramatically. Pushing up off the bed. Pushing her up with me. She had to steady herself. She threw her head back. Shook her hair wildly. And then she was still. I was panting. She waited a few moments but remained on me. Waiting for me to fade inside her. She had told me how much she liked the sensation. She reached under and fingered my balls. Now she leaned forward and kissed my ear. Nibbling at it. And then she whispered.

—Now you know what you're going to be missing.

Without another word, she got off me. In the half-light, I could see her bend down and pick up the towel. She dragged it casually along the floor as she walked away from me. The door opened bathing her beautiful body in the brightness from the hallway. She looked over at me one last time. I gazed at her beautiful shoulders, arse, and legs. And then she was gone.

Sleepy Love.

Neither asleep, nor awake,
I seem to be.
Yet in waking dreams,
You come to me.
The softest touch,
My body feels.
Your fingertips,
Like silky wheels.
No sound, no talk,
Just silent dark.
Towards you now,
My body arcs.
Then your body,
Complete and whole,
Fills my being,
Mind and soul.
We reach together,
Heaven sent.
Arrive together,
And then, we're spent.
As pillow bound,
I am once more,
Asleep? Awake?
I'm still not sure.

Written for Lauren. What a fucking fool I am!

Susan

Phillip lived about twenty minutes away from *Remains To Be Seen*. It was a nice drive and one I knew well. I lived just a mile or two away from him and took the same main road to my house in Walton Ridge.

This proximity had the promise of being both very good and *very* bad.

Good in that I could easily swing by to discuss the silver collection I had convinced him to start.

And bad, in fact downright naughty, because it could become dangerous. Dropping in often for sex. If that's where all this was going to lead. And I knew enough about myself to know that I could have Phillip if I wanted to. Unless Phillip was gay. And I was pretty certain he wasn't. That would be a nice challenge in itself though.

It was a Monday. The shop was closed and I was at home. I came out of my bathroom to the sound of Mozart's *Lacrimosa* playing downstairs. James was no doubt in his den—listening to his music and flipping through the morning papers for the third time. His habit. Mr. Predictable. James is the kind of man who breaks out occasionally and wears brown shoes. He thinks it's really fun.

A clock somewhere in the house struck 12:00. I was going to Phillip's on the pretext of taking over a set of spoons. I had carried the small box upstairs to my bedroom to examine them while I was getting ready. Maybe today would be the day. An *afternoon delight* no less.

I stood in front of the vanity mirror and took my moisturizer from a drawer. It was from Paris. I loved it but was getting dangerously low. The good news was that I would be in Paris in March for the Spring Antiques Fair. I would buy more. The daffodils would already be coming up in the *Jardin Tuileries*. People would be out in the sidewalk cafés. Maybe I could convince Phillip to travel with me.

–Get real, Susan. You're married, I said aloud to my reflection.

I opened the moisturizer and took a little out with my fingers. I dabbed it into one palm and gently rubbed my hands together, spreading it evenly and started moisturizing my shoulders. I had always looked good in off-the-shoulder dresses and took special care of my upper arms.

Often, the shoulders are the first things a man will touch. Caressing them. Putting strong arms around them.

Next, my chest. I stuck my elbows out and cupped the palms of my hands under the outside of my breasts. Then I pushed my hands towards the center of my body. Pushing my breasts together and upwards. I massaged them in gentle circular motions. I loved watching my nipples get hard. I stopped for a moment and took one of the spoons from the box. I laid it down carefully on the dresser. Taking another dab of moisturizer, I patted it behind my knees. Rubbing it into the soft skin between the ligaments. It always turned me on. A close friend, a woman, had first showed me the pleasures of it. She called it *wet behind the knees*. And sure enough, my legs always buckled.

This was a prelude to masturbating. I steadied myself against the dresser with one hand and picked up the spoon. Turning it so the underneath of the rounded bowl was facing upwards, I glided it between my legs, letting the coldness of the silver rub against me. I wasn't going to insert it. Simply rub the smoothness of its underside against my clitoris. Back and forth. Watching myself in the mirror.

I leaned forward and kissed my image, pretending I was kissing someone else. Phillip. Another woman. It didn't matter. It felt real. Lovely. I came. A long, deep wave. And then another. And then it was time to stop. I had to get ready, but now I was prepared for Phillip. I spoke to myself as I put a simple, silver chain around my neck and quickly buttoned my silk blouse.

—Now then, Phillip. I shall keep this spoon back and one day tell you the whole story. Reveal its complete and detailed history.

I laughed. I was happy. I skipped down the stairs.

Mozart had gone quiet. James had the midday news hour on. The local channel. All the usual rubbish, breathlessly broadcast as breaking stories. Slanted reporting and personal opinion masquerading as news. I kissed him on the forehead. He looked up and sniffed the air gently.

—You smell nice.

I stopped in my tracks. James never paid me compliments. Had I overdone the perfume? Was I already giving myself away? Even before I had experienced the pleasure of Phillip?

—Thank you, James. What a sweet thing to notice.

—Where are you toddling off to?

—I have to quickly deliver some spoons to a new customer, I lied. It was true I was delivering spoons, but there would be nothing quick about my visit to Phillip, other than dropping my drawers. —Then a bit of shopping. After that, I'll swing by the shop to spend time with Sarah. It's inventory week.

—I'll see you at dinner then?

—Yes. Bye, James.

—Bye bye.

I felt a little unnerved.

I backed the Range Rover out of the driveway, its tires crunching over the gravel. A sound I always associated with England and long driveways leading up to grand county houses.

Out on Aylesbury Road, I made a right and followed the main street through Walton Ridge. On the other side of town was Banbury Road. A sharp left this time. I followed the winding country lane until I saw his house. He had described it perfectly.

—It'll be on your left. Circular driveway. Farmhouse colonial. Barn red. Lots of different levels—they added on over the years, I suppose. Adjoining garage and parking to the right. It's charming.

And it was charming. Just like Phillip. I turned into the driveway and pulled into a parking space next to Phillip's Audi Estate. I heard a dog barking. Phillip opened the front door as I got out of the car. I picked up the box of spoons and put them under my arm. I was uncharacteristically nervous. A first-date kind of feeling.

—Hi, Susan.

—Hello, Phillip.

—Come in, please. Don't mind the dog. His name is J.C.

I went into the house. The dog, as they tend to, shoved his nose straight between my legs. He had a good sniff around.

—J.C. Stop that! Sorry, Susan. Do you always have that effect on boys? Phillip asked with a naughty twinkle in his eyes.

I tried to brush the dog away but he came back for more. Phillip was enjoying this.

—So what does J.C. stand for? Jesus Christ?

Phillip laughed.

—Actually, yes. A friend of mine called me and told me about a dog at the pound. That he was going to be put down. She sent me a picture of him. And that was it—I rescued him.

I was quite moved by a gentle side of Phillip that I was seeing for the first time. An animal lover. The double entendre struck me. An animal lover, I liked that. I tried to stroke the dog's head and pull his nose out of my crotch at the same time.

—But why J.C?

—Well, I was saying my prayers the night before I got him and I said, Oh by the way, God, I'm getting a dog tomorrow. Any ideas for a name?

—And then there was a flash of lightening and Jesus Christ appeared before you.

Phillip looked very slightly hurt. I instantly realized I shouldn't have teased. I didn't know him well enough, but then he smiled.

—Something like that. I stood up from praying and said to myself: Jesus Christ, Phillip! Can't you even name your own dog without asking God for help? And that was it. Jesus Christ. J.C.

I hadn't expected this of Phillip.

—So you're religious, Phillip?

—I'm not sure what you mean by that. If you mean by religious, do I go to church every Sunday, the answer is no. But I have a Higher Power. Unfortunately that doesn't always help me lead a perfect life.

Phillip looked at me intently. My legs felt wobbly again. Another *wet behind the knees* moment. He continued the thought.

—I have, for instance, been known to covet other men's wives.

The dog had lost interest in me. He went off wagging his tail. Phillip had hit the flirtation ball to my side of the court. I hit it back. I glanced at Phillip over my shoulder with my best *come fuck me* look as I took in the room.

—Oh, really? We must discuss that sometime.

The house was actually more of a cottage. It was very Phillip. The front door opened straight into the dining room in true colonial-style. A candelabrum hung in the middle of the ceiling; rescued wrought iron fashioned into a colonial-style piece. Real candles. A long pine table dominated the room, sitting on a beautiful needlepoint rug in the Persian style. There was room for a small pine side table and that was about it. The big contrast was that Phillip had added a stylish flair to this: black leather office chairs in place of regular dining room chairs. To the right, through an open doorway, was the kitchen. To the left, I could see into the living room with its beamed ceiling and wide-plank wood flooring. You could have been in England. I could smell wood smoke. Phillip had a fire going. Music was playing in the distance somewhere. Slow, sexy, 1940s jazz. Phillip squeezed by me. I caught his smell. He was wood-smoky too. A lumberjack.

–You smell nice, he said beating me to the comment I was going to make about him. And it was the second time today I had heard it. First my husband. And now my…my newest customer. That's right. That's what he was. All he was at this point.

–Thank you. What a sweet thing to notice, I said, using the exact words I had said to James. They just tumbled out of my mouth. Get a grip, girl. –I was going to say the same about you, Phillip.

He smiled. –Would you like some wine? White for this time of day?

–That's perfect, Phillip.

I heard the pop of a cork. A new bottle.

Phillip

She was wearing a dark blue silk blouse and a matching dark blue skirt, cut just on the knee. She had on just a little jewelry. Maybe they were pieces she had bought originally for the shop but decided to keep for her own collection. A simple silver chain around her neck. Antique earrings. An Art Deco ring. She took the wine I offered and looked at me over the top of her glass as she tasted it.

–Very nice.

–A *Sauvignon blanc*, I said.

–Yes. Aren't you joining me?

–I don't drink, Susan. I'll join you in spirit, as it were.

Susan raised her glass.

–In spirit then.

I had always found her so easy to talk to in the shop. But now we were here, alone in my house, on my turf, somehow there was an awkwardness. Knowing that our friendship had taken a step forward that both of us were unsure how to deal with. First-time lovers.

As if reading my mind, she put down her glass and stepped towards me. Her perfume filled my senses. She rested her hands on my shoulders and kissed me very gently on the lips. Then her hands went around my neck, gently stroking the back of it. I slid my hands around her waist and pulled her closer to me. We kissed again, this time deeper, longer. My hands glided from around her waist and up over her breasts. We both knew what we wanted. She had made it easy to do away with the formalities. I slowly undid her blouse. She was wearing a black silk bra. I bent down and kissed the tops of her breasts. The skin had lost some of the elasticity of her youth. But there was the softness and fullness that only comes with the passing of years. I removed her blouse. And then I slid the straps of her bra down over her shoulders, at the same time, unclasping it. It fell away to reveal her nipples. She had undone my shirt and was kissing my chest.

My hand worked its way up the inside of her skirt. All the way up her stockings—real stockings—until it came to a band of soft flesh. I continued up, feeling the edge of her panties. I worked my forefinger inside the elastic, feeling her velvety hair, gently massaging her. Her back stiffened, thrusting her hips hard against mine. I felt her hand rubbing over the front of my pants, anxiously tugging at my belt. I kissed her deeply again and then pulled back.

–There's a fire in the sitting room.

–Is there now? A fire. Yes, fire would be nice, Phillip.

Heavenly Half-Hour.

Thirty minutes,
One half-hour.
Eighteen hundred seconds,
We devour.

Stolen moments
Are what we have.
In between this,
We grab some of that.

No coffee or sandwiches,
On our lunch break.
It's off with our clothes
And make no mistake.

Sometimes it's only
A telephone call,
But total nudity
Is our Golden Rule.

Of one thing we're certain,
This love we have found.
Squeezed into thirty minutes
Is a love without bounds.

Phillip

We made love at my house. And that really should have been the end of it.

I kept telling myself I only responded to Susan's overtures because…well…because she was making them.

What's a boy to do?

A beautiful mature woman practically throwing herself at him? And it was all entirely safe. She was married. I was freshly divorced. No want or need of a relationship on either part. Just good, old-fashioned sex. Susan called it an *afternoon delight*. And that's what it should have been. A delightful one-off bonk.

But the sex with Susan had awakened something in me. A stirring in the loins as my old dad would have said. But it was more than that. It was like a drink for me. One was too many; a thousand wouldn't be enough. I craved her already. I also liked her.

There were none of the usual thoughts following lovemaking with Susan. As much as I hated myself for it, I found myself rather impatient with some women I fucked.

–What are you hanging around for? We've just fucked. It was great but I need some alone time now.

Well, maybe not quite *that* ungentlemanly.

But after we had made love, I wanted Susan to stay. To linger in my bed. To talk. I wanted us to touch each other some more. Lay in each other's arms.

She talked about things I didn't know about. She came from a different world. And she was genuinely interested in my world and me. Beyond the sex.

Stimulating in every sense.

Now she was sitting naked on the rumpled sheets. Her knees tucked under her chin. Her arms cuddling her shins. She formed a perfect hourglass shape. She was swaying gently from side to side. Her ankles and calves, at first pulled together, opened slightly with each sway allowing me delicious glimpses of her pubic hairs, starting where her bum ended and where her beautiful vagina began. She knew she was showing me this most intimate view of herself and made no attempt to hide it. Her head was looking down, towards her feet, but her eyes were looking up from under her eyelids.

So sexy.

Her skin was glowing. Her hair was ruffled from where I had first run my fingers gently through it and then pulled at it—pulling her head backwards during our lovemaking, pushing her lower body into me in the same action.

In this sitting position, her breasts were squeezed against her thighs. Flattening them out. Quarter moons balanced on each side of her luscious legs. I imagined her nipples again. Dark against the whiteness of her fantastic tits.

I raised myself up, tucked my lower legs under, and sat up straight in a kneeling position opposite her. I rested my hands palm down on my thighs. I turned them over. She watched my every move. I brought my hands up to her shoulders. Every part of me was tingling. I put my hands either side of her neck and smoothed her shoulders in repeated gliding motions. My fingertips were barely, just barely, touching her skin. She closed her eyes and raised her chin, arching her neck like a cat arches its back when you stroke it.

–That's delicious. Don't stop, Phillip.

I didn't. She stopped swaying though and sat perfectly still. Concentrating on my hands. Enjoying the moment.

–You've got beautifully soft shoulders, Susan.

–Thank you. I try to look after them.

The only sound entering the room was the distant strain of Betty Carter coming from downstairs.

After our first round of lovemaking earlier in the sitting room, on the rug in front of the fire, we dressed and attempted to turn to the business at hand, the reason Susan had supposedly come over in the first place: to discuss my silver collection. It didn't take much convincing that I should start one. Just like Susan, I saw it as a means of constant contact with each other. We had spread the silver Fiddle pattern dessertspoons over the dining room table.

–These are all from 1822 through 1826. Scottish.

I couldn't help myself. I was in puerile schoolboy form.

–Yes, they're exquisite spoons. But I suppose a fork's out of the question?

She had started to reply that she could get matching forks before collapsing into laughter at my awful pun.

–I'd love to fork you again, Phillip. Yes, why not?

For the second time that afternoon, we found ourselves naked but now in my bedroom. I watched her enjoy my light touch as I caressed her, and I became erect again.

She didn't open her eyes but must have sensed it. She laid both hands gently on my hard cock. Very softly gliding them up and down, like a potter quietly molding damp, moist clay into a tall vase. I got harder and taller too.

She opened her eyes.

–I love your cock, Phillip. It's beautiful.

–Really? I don't have a lot to compare it to.

She laughed.

–Trust me. It's beautiful.

Her thighs parted again, allowing me a clear view of her pussy. She was entirely comfortable sitting there naked and just started chatting as if we were in a café somewhere. The confidence of an older woman.

–So when did you lose your virginity?

–My virginity?

–Yes. I'm assuming you were a virgin once.

–Well, yes. I lost it a long time ago. I was *just* sixteen.

–At least you were sixteen! But still a baby.

–I thought I was rather grown up actually. I had a good

growth of pubic hair and my *beautiful cock* as you just put it. All I had to do was put it to good use.

–And you did! Tell me about it. What was her name?

Susan lay back on the bed and rested against the pillow. The soft feathers molding themselves to her head. She spread her arms and legs. Against the pure white sheets, she looked like a child making an angel in the snow. Hiding absolutely nothing. I was still kneeling between her feet, looking down at her, my cock stiff.

–Valerie Barrington-Bird. She was my first older woman.

Susan raised her eyebrows.

–Your first was an older woman?

–She was seventeen.

Susan laughed out loud.

–Well at that age, sixteen, I suppose a year older did make her the mature type you would come to love all your life. Wasn't your wife older than you?

–Yes. By a few years, but I don't want her in my bed now. Let's concentrate on Valerie.

–Yes, let's. What did she look like?

–She was tall and thin. This was the early seventies and all the girls wanted to look like Vogue models. She had that typical boyish bob of a haircut and wore lots of black eye-make up. I remember her big soft lips. She could easily have been a runway star. Very pretty.

–Do you have any pictures of her?

–Susan, this was years ago.

–Well, I'm starting to get very horny. I want to have an exact picture in my head.

–Do you like girls, Susan?

–I have been known to like what you like, Phillip, but let's save that for another occasion. Okay. So she's tall, a swinging dolly bird. Mini-skirt. Tight sweater. Seventeen-year-old boobs. Was Valerie a virgin?

–I didn't ask. I don't think so. She seemed to know what she was doing. I met her at a party. She was dancing with my friend, Jim, and I was dancing with her friend, Diane.

Diane had a father-imposed curfew and had to leave, so I walked her home, acted gentlemanly, and went back to the party to see if there was any other action. Jim was drunk and Valerie didn't want to dance with him anymore. She asked me if I'd walk her home.

—Good Lord. You were walking all over that night.

—Yes, but *this* walk was worth it. We got to her house and…

Susan raised her arms as if to welcome me into an embrace. I pushed myself over and lay down on top of her. She whispered in my ear.

—I want you to call me Valerie. Keep saying it. I'm going to be the one you lose your virginity to all over again. What happened next?

—I kissed her. I thought it would just be goodnight.

Susan put her hands lightly around my head. She held on very gently and let her fingertips run through my hair. Barely touching me. She kissed me. And then suddenly she was Valerie.

—Phillip, would you like to come in? My mum and dad are asleep upstairs, we'll have to be quiet.

—I'll be quiet, Valerie.

—What happened then?

—Valerie led me into her sitting room. There were no lights and we bumped into a chair. She said, Shhh! She pulled me onto the sofa. It was completely dark. We necked.

Susan was Valerie again.

—Phillip, I can feel your cock against me. How old are you?

—Sixteen.

—If we do this, Phillip, it has to be our secret. You're a whole year younger than me. I don't want my friends to know I slept with a kid. Promise?

—I promise, Valerie.

Susan/Valerie slid her hands down my body. She pretended she was unbuckling a belt and then unzipping my fly. She put her hand flat on my stomach and slid it downwards, as if sliding her hand inside imaginary underpants.

She fumbled around my balls. She was acting out my moment of sexual maturity with precision, undressing me even though I was already totally naked.

–Oh, Valerie.

–Shhh! You'll wake my dad. Don't take your trousers all the way off in case he comes down. You can put your hand up my sweater but I'm not taking it off, just in case.

I slid my hand along Susan/Valerie's body as if sliding it under a sweater. My hand reached her breast. I pretended that my hand had to find its way under a bra. I squeezed her nipples gently.

–Ahhhh.

Susan/Valerie guided my cock towards her pussy.

–Phillip. You're about to lose your virginity. And you always remember your first. Are you ready for this?

–Yes, Valerie

Susan/Valerie pulled me expertly inside. I came instantly.

–Whoa, Phillip! Is that all you gave Valerie? Two strokes and a load of the good stuff?

–Susan! That's shocking talk. Anyway, I was just sixteen for Christ's sake.

–Yeah, but I was expecting something that lasted a little longer. Now that you've had a bit of experience.

–Well, you did it. Your pussy had complete control over me just then.

–I can have that effect on men, yes.

–Well all I can say is, take control.

Susan laughed her lovely laugh.

–Did you ever see Valerie again?

–Yes. At the library. She smiled at me but had this look on her face as if she were trying to place me. Trying to figure out where she knew me from.

Susan started to sing.

–*Unforgettable. That's what you are.*

I hit her over the head with a pillow. And then we made love again.

Susan

When I got back that evening, I was surprised to find that James had made dinner. He didn't normally cook. The joke was that he didn't even know where the kitchen was. And we'd been here one way or another for more than thirty years.

My parents had owned the house originally.

They came to America in the 1970s while I was still in London working in advertising.

My father worked as a Brand Director for Universal Foods in the U.K. Before it became part of Lenz Foods and before Lenz Foods became part of a big tobacco concern. He was getting to that age when no one quite knew what to do with him.

He had done a good job for Universal Foods, introducing famous American brands to the finicky world of British marketing.

The big brass didn't want to force him out but the day had come when younger faces were wanted around the place. People more in tune with the social revolution from London's swinging sixties that was having a ripple effect into the seventies. An effect on the way people spoke, dressed, and even ate.

Dad just wasn't *with it* as the period's pop stars had urged everyone to be.

And so he was offered a special job. He would be Worldwide Coordinator of Universal Foods Global Brands working out of the White Plains, New York headquarters. In other words, as he put it, he sat in front of a huge map of the world with the Universal logo plastered all over it, and if any visitor asked where UF sold its products, Dad was your man. Kuala Lumpur? Yeah, you can buy Foyer's Ice Cream there.

Other than that, he did bugger all. Apart from improving his golf game at the swanky Chester Country Club where he entertained the heads of the Universal Foods divisions from as far away as Australia.

Dad had drawn a thirty-mile radius on a map around White Plains in an attempt to narrow down a town where they might want to live and which would be a relatively easy commute to the office. Mum was aghast to find that the circle overlapped to the west into parts of New Jersey. She had never been there but an American friend had given her preconceived ideas.

—More like the *Asshole State* than the *Garden State*, her friend had put it.

Mum wanted nothing to do with it after that despite dad telling her that he was sure it was just a dangerous generalization.

To the south was Manhattan. The lure of the theatre and nightlife was all very appealing but she couldn't imagine living in a city after the bucolic joys of English country living for all those years. And certainly not a city on the verge of bankruptcy, which is what New York was in the '70s.

To the east was the Connecticut coastline. Seaside living didn't appeal. And so it was to the north they ventured.

To Walton Ridge.

The house sat on about seven acres and the seven acres sat on the edge of a picturesque lake. The house had been built in the 1920s as part of a lake community. Originally the houses were quite small—they were summer and weekend homes for New York City dwellers—but in the same way that electrification of the train line made towns like Old Woodford directly accessible from the city with its own train station, villages like Walton Ridge also became desirable. These villages were just a twenty minute drive from the train station and property values skyrocketed. Mum and dad bought at the right time. Their property was even more special because it also boasted a guesthouse.

Over the years, both the main house and guesthouse

were enlarged and now were both quite lovely. When I announced that James had suddenly been offered a super duper job on Wall Street and that we were coming to America, it was only natural that the guesthouse would be offered to us as a place to live while we were looking for a home of our own.

Dad's position as head of the world was short-lived. When Lenz Foods took over Universal Foods, they didn't have the same sentimentality for dad as his London bosses. The Lenz Foods bean counters simply saw him as an outdated, unnecessary waste of resources sitting in a big office, where he put in hours practicing his golf swing and not much more. Even dad could see they were right. He had got rid of a version of himself during a similar cost-cutting operation in London.

Dad's retirement coincided with my mother's illness. By the mid-seventies, the American Cancer Society was screening women for breast cancer in a project called *Breast Cancer Detection Demonstration*. Mum was encouraged by her new American friends to take advantage of this and discovered she had late stage breast cancer. She was dead within six months. Dad died shortly after. No need to live, as he put it.

So we never moved away; we simply moved across the garden and into the main house. The guesthouse became Sarah's years later when she came to the States.

—*Roast chicken, fingerling potatoes with parsley butter, and salad.*

—Goodness, James. What has got into you? Cooking? It smells so good.

—Well, you stirred the old boy up this morning. *You* smelled so good. Your perfume. I thought I would wine and dine you, and you never know where it might lead. Maybe even up to Bedfordshire!

—James! You silly old sausage.

I had spent the entire afternoon fucking Phillip; I come home and now my husband was horny as hell as well. I threw my coat over a kitchen chair.

—I need a shower. Do I have time before dinner?

James turned from the kitchen counter and handed me a glass of white wine.

—A *Sauvignon blanc,* he said.

—Oh, thank you, I said somewhat startled. Déjà vu all over again. I couldn't quite believe this.

—Yes, you have time to shower. Dinner will be ready in about thirty minutes. Take a bath if you want.

—I think I will, yes. Thank you, James.

I walked through to the dining room that sat at an angle to the kitchen. It used to be a screened-in porch but my parents winterized it. Now the haphazard slant of the room added to the lovely charm of the house. French doors led into the main room with its stone fireplace and wood floors. Large windows opened up to a view of the lake. I loved this house. A small flight of stairs led to the bedroom. I had decorated it very simply. There was a sleigh bed from the turn of the twentieth century; small bedside tables, an upholstered rocker, an oak blanket chest, and the vanity where I had been vain enough to kiss myself in the mirror. I smiled.

I shed my clothes. No knickers though. Phillip had kept them—a memento, he said. I quite enjoyed the feeling driving home. I had lifted my skirt up when I climbed in the Range Rover and Phillip hoisted it further still. My bare arse made contact with the finest quality Connolly leather. It was delicious. My body was already all aquiver from the fucking and the feeling of the Range Rover's seat against my skin only served to rev me up some more. Phillip wanted to fuck in the car, there and then. But that would have to be saved for another day I told him. Besides, as I said, I don't do stuff like that.

—Maybe you do now, he had said with a sparkling smile.

I ran hot water into the claw-foot tub in my bathroom. James's bathroom was down the hall. We both liked and enjoyed our privacy. I took my bubble bath from the shelf alongside the tub. *Penhaligon's Cabbage Rose.* So very English.

I loved Penhaligon's and always stocked up when I went back to England. You could buy it in New York but it wasn't the same as bringing it back from the U.K. The bottle had a long, slender neck. I ran my hands along the smoothness of the glass. A hard prick. Yum. I uncorked the bottle and poured a liberal measure of the sweet-smelling liquid into the bath.

I pulled my hair back into a ponytail, took off my necklace and ring, and slipped into the warm water. The bubbles fought eagerly to climb up my breasts. I swished the water around and let my warm hand rest between my legs. I washed my pussy.

It reminded me of the old joke about the mum who caught her son masturbating in the bath. When she told him to stop, he simply exclaimed: It's my willy and I'll wash it as fast as I want.

It's my pussy and I'll wash it as fast as I want.

I'd like to take a bath with Phillip, I thought to myself and closed my eyes. Just for a moment...

—Wakey, wakey.

I sat up, startled. James was standing casually in the doorway, holding his evening whisky.

—I'm sorry to barge into your bathroom but you didn't answer when I called you for dinner. It's ready.

—Oh, James. I'm sorry, I must have dozed off.

—A busy afternoon. The inventory with Sarah and what have you. You must be really tired.

—Yes, very busy. Hand me that towel, will you?

I had known this man for more than thirty years but suddenly I was embarrassed to be naked in front of him. I wasn't sure quite why. James handed me the towel and looked me up and down. Nothing seemed to register.

Phillip had admired me. Told me I had a beautiful body. Made me feel sexy.

If James was feeling horny, he had a strange way of showing it. Despite all his plans for wining and dining.

—I'll see you downstairs, he said.

—Yes, I won't be a mo.

I went back into the bedroom and threw on a long satiny dress. No underwear. I liked this new *nay knickers* thing a lot. I decided to go barefoot as well. The hem of the dress tickled my feet lusciously as I padded across the rug and down to dinner.

I have to say, the dinner was delicious.

—You should cook more often, James.

I indicated flirtatiously with a nod in the vague direction of the bedroom.

—Maybe I will, yes.

Beethoven was playing now, the *Pastoral* drifting through from James's study. The candles were burning low. The dress fell nicely between my legs. I had my hands in my lap.

I squeezed them between my thighs, pulling at the satin. I was very aware of my nipples. Erect. James peeked over. It was one of those surreptitious looks men always give women across a table—a quick glance at the old tits and then back up again before you get caught.

—Well, Susan, I should do the dishes.

I stood up, smoothed my dress pulling it tight over my breasts. I walked slowly around the table, my eyes fixed on James the whole time. I stood behind him and let my hands glide over his shoulders. And then I let my fingers run lightly down his spine. I slipped my hands under his arms and reached through to his chest. I massaged him as I bent down and kissed him gently on the neck. It was all very soft. And very silent. His head went up and I kissed his ear and whispered to him.

—I'll do the dishes. You go up and get ready.

I trailed my hand lazily across his shoulders as I leaned forward to blow out the candles. My body brushed against his arm. The smell of the hot candle wax filled my nostrils. It was a smell I loved. The end of an evening downstairs. The start of one upstairs.

James got up from the table and headed upstairs. I quickly gathered up the dishes. I wanted sex. I pretended to be appalled at myself for not caring who it was with. James, Phillip, or anyone else for that matter. I just wanted to get laid again. I was hornier than the high school band, as they say, despite the stupendous afternoon sex.

I stacked the plates in the sink, opened the fridge, took out the *Sauvignon blanc,* and poured myself another glass. The unnecessary last drink. But lovely.

I locked up and switched off all the lights. Smoke lingered lazily from the last log burning in the fireplace. It glowed red and grey in the dark, an occasional lick of flame lighting up the room.

Okay, girl. Up to Bedfordshire, as James had put it. Let's see if there are any fires burning up there. I turned off Beethoven. An unfinished symphony of my making.

By the time I got upstairs, James was already in bed. He was sitting up reading a biography of John Adams. He looked over his glasses towards me and gestured to my side of the bed. He had folded the covers back for me. Something he had done for years, a sweet gesture. He was a sweet man. But for fuck's sake, James! He wanted to get lucky and he's wearing his pajamas? His best ones admittedly, but pajamas all the same. This might take some work. I turned off the lamp on my side of the bed and walked around to his side. I stood in front of him. He put his book down, carefully marking the page. He took off his glasses and put them very deliberately on the bedside table.

He looked back at me and blinked, his eyes adjusting to suddenly being without his spectacles.

I put my left hand over my right hip and folded my right arm over the top of my left arm. I gathered up the long satin dress by continually stroking my thigh and holding on to the loose material as it collected around my waist. When the hem was within my reach, I grabbed it and pulled the dress slowly up over my thighs. I knew when the dress had revealed my pubic hairs and I let it linger there for a moment. I wanted James to see my bush, to watch me strip for him. I continued pulling until the dress came up over my breasts, my neck, and my head. In contrast to James's careful putting away of his book and glasses, I simply threw the dress down on the floor. I stepped forward and took James's face in my hands. I pulled his head into my breasts. I wanted small bites. Little nibbles. Some playful gnawing. I stroked the top of his head. James kissed my breasts without passion. Just repeated noisy kisses that sounded like he was trying to say the word *Why* over and over but couldn't quite get it out.

He pulled back.

—I'll turn out the light.

—Leave it on, James. I want to see you.

He ignored me and turned the light out anyway. I felt his hand take mine in the darkness, gesturing me into bed. I climbed over him and lay down on my side. I felt him removing his pajama bottoms. I didn't bother trying to unbutton his top. I knew this wouldn't take long. James climbed on top of me and kissed my neck and told me he loved me. I told him I loved him too. I spread my legs and helped him in.

Female army recruits in the U.K. during World War One were told part of their mission might be to sleep with the enemy. Literally. They were to gather intelligence while fucking German officers. When one woman said she couldn't possibly bed a German, she was told: *Just close your eyes and think of England.*

I closed my eyes and thought of Phillip.

A Flash of Need.

Irresistible urge,
A flash of need,
A want of love,
That won't recede.

This luscious lust,
I will allow,
Not tomorrow,
But now, right now.

My blouse unbuttoned,
Naked he lies,
I remove my skirt,
I feast my eyes.

I want him now,
Desire he feeds.
I must relieve,
This flash of need.

*Wrote this after Susan told me I made her
hornier than the high school band.*

Hmm.

I liked the last poem Phillip wrote. The one in my voice.

—*I want him now, desire he feeds.*

Phillip had already given me his front door key.

—Just let me know if you decide to drop by, he had said rather casually.

But wouldn't that spoil the surprise?

Besides, why waste precious shagging time making a phone call?

I must relieve this flash of need.

Phillip

I heard the click-clack across the landing at the top of the staircase. The low creak of the bedroom door as she pushed it open. I turned over and opened my eyes. She had stopped in the doorway and was leaning seductively against the doorframe. She was wearing a full-length fur coat.

The click-clack had come from her black high-heeled shoes. She pushed one pointed toe forward until her leg parted the front of her coat. She wanted me to see it all— ankle, calf, thigh. Long, slender, beautiful.

Her hair was up, ballet style, but she reached up, unfastened a clip, and shook it loose.

Even from here I could see her eyes sparkle with naughtiness. She walked towards me never taking her eyes off me.

She stopped again. At the end of the bed.

She glanced quickly towards the window and back at me. Teasing. She lowered her chin and opened her coat.

She was wearing nothing but a negligible négligée.

Her coat fell away to the floor.

She laid her left hand on her stomach and then slid it up over her right breast.

Her nipples under the sensual silk of the négligée were hard in an instant.

She had told me that when I kissed them, it ignited a direct electrical current to the soft meeting point at the top of her beautiful legs.

I had never wanted her more than I did that very second.

Good Morning

You faced away
And as you lay,
Your shoulders
Gently shrugged.

I turned to you,
Desire grew,
My arms around
You, hugged.

I kissed your neck,
Caressed your ear.
With words cooed,
Like a dove.

You turned around—
My body found,
And wrapped me
In your love.

A gentle kiss,
Then welded bliss,
And fire
Without warning.

Body scent and
Passions spent.
And then you said,
"Good morning."

Susan

Rather than feeling satisfied from the sex with Phillip, I just wanted more. He was on the way to the shop to pick up a carving fork. This was newer—1880s—but it would still perfectly match the Georgian set we were building for him. I assured him it would only add to the value of the total collection because it was such a nice piece. I had sent him a rather naughty fax using his own pun: If you still fancy that fork, it's waiting here for you at the shop. Completely unwrapped.

Phillip stepped into the shop and I felt the minge twinge immediately. The old nipples perked up in an instant.

His hair was slicked back, still wet from the shower. He hadn't shaved. A dark shadow framed his face. Like a construction guy. My bit of rough. He was wearing black cowboy boots, tight Levi's and a black T-shirt. He looked more like he had stepped out of a James Dean movie than a house in tony Chester County. A black cashmere overcoat hung perfectly over his beautiful body. A pale yellow cashmere scarf completed the look. He just stared at me with those suggestive, slate blue eyes. The corners of his mouth went up into a smile. He oozed sex. Pure, raw, and unmistakable. He had said a few days ago that I had total control over him. No, come to think of it, what he actually said was that my pussy had total control over him. Right now, my pussy was completely out of control. It was in utter uproar.

I walked over to him. We had said no kissing in the shop but I thought, fuck it. I wanted to kiss him. I simply had to. I locked the door behind him and flipped the *Open* sign to

Closed. I kissed him deeply. He came up for air.

—What's got into you?

—You. Well you're about to.

—What if someone peers in? What if your husband comes by?

—James wouldn't come by without calling first. He's still very formal even after all these years. His Army training. But let me show you what we'd do if he did show up.

I had planned to show this to Phillip the second or third time he stopped by the shop. But I thought better of it. Maybe that really would have been a little too forward of me.

I took Phillip's hand and we walked over to the back wall. We stood in front of it.

—What do you see, Phillip?

He looked hard.

—A wall I suppose. A picture hanging on it. The classic hunting scene that you see in every antiques shop. A mirror. Heavy. Gilt-edged with a bow. Needs re-silvering.

—Ha-ha!

—Pardon, Susan?

—Nobody would know it, but it's there. I call it the *Ha-Ha* cupboard.

Phillip

Susan touched something; I didn't see what but the wall swung back.

It revealed a cupboard-like space. It wasn't dingy or cobwebby like you'd expect a hidden recess to be. This was more like the interior of a wood-lined closet—minus the clothes. A narrow bench was built into the back wall but there was hardly room for two people to stand, yet alone sit. Susan took my hand again and led me inside. She turned me so we were facing each other, pulled the door shut, and we were plunged into darkness.

—There. A secret hiding place.

I could feel her hot breath on my neck as she snuggled up to me in the tight space.

—How did you find this? Who told you it was here?

—I found it by accident. Running my hands over the walls. A lot of houses like this from the revolutionary period had hiding places where wanted men could be hidden from the dastardly English. When the Redcoats approached, it was into the closet! The hiding place was rumored in the town historical records to be here but the previous owners said they knew nothing about it. Anyway I found it when I was looking for a stud in the wall to drill into and hang the mirror that you were just complaining about. I banged around the wall tapping the plaster, and when I hit a stud, the door suddenly opened. I would have never have found it otherwise.

—You're right. You would never know it was here. Does anyone else know about this? What about James?

—No, not James. Not that I'm keeping it from him. We just don't talk about this kind of thing. Plus this is the shop. And it's my shop. My reason for not hanging around the house all day doing nothing. The shop keeps me busy. I love buying and selling the antiques, I enjoy flying to nice places on business, and I make money. James stays out of it pretty much. As long as you're happy is all he usually says. Sarah knows about the cupboard. She was holding the hammer and hook while I was searching for a stud.

—I won't comment on that.

It was weird talking like this in the dark.

—Do you believe in ghosts, Susan?

—I don't know. Why do you ask? Because we're in a *scary, creepy closet?*

She said it like a kid would, trying to scare her younger brother.

—I just wondered if anybody had ever died in here. They hid in here and got forgotten. Or were left to rot. Or couldn't breathe because they had used up all the air.

—There's a recessed air-duct in the ceiling that vents out

through the roof. It's hidden from view outside but it's a bit of a pain when there's a heavy downpour—the rain sometimes blows in and drips into the cupboard. But who knows? Somebody may have died in here. Are you one of those people with extra intuition, who feels the other side?

–No, but my sister says she senses me—if I'm feeling happy or sad, or sick or whatever. I did meet someone in London who claimed to cross over to the other side.

–Really? Tell me.

–I had been in England on business and met an old man named Albert at a party. He claimed to see things other people can't see. We were just chatting and he glanced away. When he turned back, his brown eyes turned black as coal, and he seemed to go into a trance. Suddenly he said there was a lady standing next to me with silver hair and a white streak running up from her widow's peak. She had her arm around my shoulders. He described my mum perfectly. Mum died years before. July, 1983. Then he told me a little girl was running towards me. She needed my help.

–Did you know who he meant?

–No, I told him I couldn't think who she might be. He looked away again, and when he turned back, his eyes were blacker still. He said the girl's name was Celestia. Not a common name. Celestia is my goddaughter, Susan. Albert didn't know me, had never seen a picture of my mum, and certainly didn't know I had a goddaughter, let alone that her name was the unusual Celestia. Albert told me things about myself that night that only I would know.

–Wow, Phillip. That's spooky. So did you ask him, you know, how long you would live?

–You mean, when would I die? He wouldn't tell me. He was ambiguous, all he said was, –You are destined.

–Don't worry, Phillip. I won't let any harm come to you. I'll hold you very tightly.

And then she squeezed my nuts.

–Oh, I think I've found the stud again.

I kissed her. I spoke into her ear.

—You were Valerie a few days ago. It's my turn to act. Who do you want me to be? Imagine somebody, anybody you'd like to kiss. Real or made up. Alive or dead. Doesn't matter. We're in the dark so I can be that person.

Susan laughed and then whispered.

—I want you to pretend you're a woman. A young girl. It's your turn be Valerie.

—I like it. Right you are, Susan. Valerie it is.

I found Susan's face in the dark and held her. I guided her towards my lips. I put the very tip of my tongue in the very corner of my mouth. A little nub of soft, pink flesh sticking out from my lips.

Susan kissed me and gasped.

—That felt like I was kissing a clitoris.

—You obviously know.

—My lesbian experiment as a young girl. Let me kiss you—it—again. That was lovely.

This time Susan expertly licked the tip of my tongue, running her lips over the edges of my lips. It tickled and tingled. She was experiencing the same sensation. I put my hand up her skirt and let it linger between her legs.

—Oh, my god, Phillip. This really *is* just like licking clit. Where did you get this idea?

—I just made it up. I thought you'd like it.

—I do.

Susan dropped to her knees in the tight space. In a single move, she had my cock out. The inside of her mouth felt soft and fuzzy, like a peach. She raised and lowered her lips in a slow, easy rhythm.

I came. She came, just from what she was doing to me. She wiggled back up and I held her close.

—Tell me more about your lesbian experiments.

She was silent for a moment. Then she spoke, quietly and almost wistfully.

—Well, it was actually only one. I was a one woman, woman, Phillip. It was wonderful. But then it got difficult— I had just got married. Fortunately, it was also about the time I moved to the States. Years later, she got in touch with me again and moved here herself. She said she had never gotten over it.

–Did you see her again? Here? What was her name?

–Sarah. It was Sarah, Phillip.

–Your Sarah? Sarah who looks after the shop? She was your boss once, right?

–Yes, that's right. And now we're friends. Old friends.

I remained silent in the dark. So Susan fucked Sarah, eh? I could see that. Sarah was still very attractive but she must have been beautiful when she was younger. I tried to imagine them in bed together. My thoughts were disturbed by the sound of Susan pushing the door open. Light flooded into the room as we emerged from our cocoon.

–Does James know about Sarah?

–No. I don't think so. No, I'm sure he doesn't. And he never will, Phillip.

Hands that see.

My hands
Search the dark,
Like a flashlight
In the night.
Feeling your body,
My fingers
Are my sight.
My hands are candles,
Burning bright.
And when they touch
Your softest skin,
My hands my mind
Excites.

*Susan, you can keep me in
the dark anytime!*

Phillip

Susan was on my mind at every turn. I kept forgetting to do things.

I hadn't been to the post office for days to get my mail. I paid cursory attention to my personal emails. Susan and I didn't send each other online messages. She wasn't really into it. Preferring a fax that could be torn up with no trace. I forgot to pay the cleaning ladies and they went on strike. I ignored voicemail messages from my friends.

I'm living in a kind of daydream, as Nat King Cole put it.

I was still getting my work done though. Just. I provided advice to entrepreneurs. I had a good reputation. My website told the world that I...*Bring to life the great ideas that might have otherwise gathered dust.* I analyzed the marketplace. Wrote business plans. And then when a product took off, I was part of engineering its sale to a big concern.

I made good money. Enough to indulge myself in a silver collection as a means of indulging myself in a relationship with a wonderful but very married woman. Three Hail Marys. You're a bad, bad boy, Phillip.

The phone rang and I knew I should answer without even looking at caller ID. It would be my sister. My beautiful twin. Hollywood calling.

–Jen?

–Holy fuck. You're alive. What the hell has been going on? You haven't answered any of my emails!

–Sorry. They're piling up. I'm only attending to business at the moment.

The phone went quiet. Then Jennifer laughed.

–What kind of business, Phillip? The kind that involves

a big pair of tits and a pussy?

—You're disgusting.

—Thank you, brother. Seriously, Phillip. You can't go silent on me. All I could think was that you were dating Mrs. bloody Smirnoff again. That you were flat on your back drunk somewhere. Out cold. Like last time. Please don't do that to me. You know how much I love you.

—I know, Jen. I'm sorry.

—So, Phillip. Are you dating Mrs. Smirnoff again?

—No, Jen. I've been sober eleven months now. I'm very happy. In a good place. I haven't thought about drinking. I love my sponsor.

—His name is Phillip as well, right?

—Yeah. I figured if I relapsed, at least I wouldn't forget his name. There is a different Mrs. in my life now though. And I *have* been flat on my back with her.

—Oh no, not a married woman!

—I'm afraid so, Jen.

—The last time we spoke you said you were done with married women, Phillip.

—I was talking about my ex-wife, you twit.

Jen laughed.

—I know, I know. So what's it all about? Tell your sister.

—I met her. I fancied her. She fancied me. We shagged. And now I want her more.

—Oh, brother. Thanks for the enlightenment. Do you mean you want more as in a relationship? Would this Mrs. ever leave her Mr. for you, Phillip?

—Well, yes. No. She would never leave her husband. I don't think. But who knows? That remains to be seen.

Jennifer said, *Huh!* and it was full of sarcasm.

—Another one of your answers laden with clarity, Phillip. Here's a simple question. Where do you do your shagging?

—My house. Her shop after closing time. She owns an antiques store.

—Her shop? Are you nuts? What if someone—like her *husband* stopped by? What would you do? Hop in the closet?

I laughed out loud. Jen's intuition was always spot on.

—Ha! Ha! Something like that. More of a cupboard. A hidden cupboard. One her husband doesn't know about. Talking of closets, have you come out?

—Well...yes and no. I like girls but I still like men. Although with the last few, it was either feast or fucking famine.

—What do you mean? Feast or famine?

—Well there was one guy who must have been taking Viagra or something. He used to get hard as hell.

—What's wrong with that?

—It was for *two hours* at a bloody time, Phillip! And he never seemed to come. It was fun at first but then I would get exhausted. He was like the fucking Energizer Bunny.

—Jesus, Jennifer! And the famine?

—The one with nothing at all. One inch and twelve wrinkles. I politely suggested one of those penis pumps and I never heard from him again.

—I think I'd stick with pussy if I were you.

—Yes, I think I will. And besides, in my eyes, no man ever lives up to my darling brother.

—Ah, Jen. You say the nicest things.

A car came in the driveway and disappeared into the garage. The dog started barking.

—I hear J.C. How's he doing, Phillip?

—Great. He follows me everywhere. He even waits outside the door when I'm in the bathroom and then spins around and around excitedly when I come out. As if I had gone away forever. He seems knows exactly where I am at all times.

—I wish I did, Phillip.

—I'm fine, Jen. Really. I'm sober. I'm not thinking about drinking. I'm happy. And I've got to go.

—Stay in touch. Otherwise I'll fly out and shred your dick with a cheese grater.

—Ouch, sister. I love you.

—I love you too, darling boy.

Susan

It was Sunday afternoon. James was playing golf. I slipped over to Phillip's.

Instead of using the front door key, Phillip was now leaving the garage open and I drove straight in. I shut the door behind me. I went into the house through the garage. No one could tell I was there. Safer.

We made love.

And then we lay in each other's arms. A gentle breeze came in through the open window. The winter sun lit up the lace curtains throwing crocheted patterns across the floor. It was peaceful. A moment of serenity. Phillip closed his eyes.

I ran my finger from his forehead, along his beautiful nose, and let it rest on his lips.

–Tell me something I don't know about you.

Phillip turned his head towards me and opened his eyes.

–I'm an alcoholic.

Phillip

I hadn't told my story to many people. My family and close friends knew. It was painful to reveal it all. I was ashamed of it, but at the same time I always felt a sense of relief at having shared it, having opened up. I looked at Susan. I wanted to be honest, but didn't want to scare her away either.

–Are you sure you really want to hear this?

She looked at me, her eyes seemed full of compassion. And that's when I realized I loved her. That was the moment when it started becoming more than an affair for me.

–Yes, Phillip. Tell me.

–You'd better get comfortable. This will take a bit of time.

I stretched my arm across her pillow. She snuggled into

my armpit and I held her close. I kissed her forehead.

And then I began.

—*I drank heavily all my life. You know what it was like in England in the seventies. Three-hour lunches. The more you could knock back in one session, the more of a hero you were. I brought all those habits to America.*

My marriage started to fall apart. I had an affair. I became a part-time father.

After a particularly heavy drinking bout, I finally checked into rehab and it seemed very successful. I stayed sober for several months. But I didn't enroll in an after-care program. I relapsed. I secretly started drinking a bottle of vodka a day. Then one or two bottles. Lauren and I split up and I moved into this house. By the time my sister came to visit for a couple of days, I had poisoned my system. I couldn't drink while she was there. I shook a lot instead.

I was always making excuses about my drinking. Business and financial pressures. Work frustrations. Then my marriage problems. Always someone else or something else to blame except taking responsibility myself.

Jennifer went back to L.A. I was functioning again but I wasn't well. I still hadn't had a drink since Jennifer left that morning. More than two whole days. I had a CD playing in the background. The phone rang and I turned the music off so I could hear the person on the other end of the line. I'm deaf in one ear.

Susan looked at me quizzically.

—You are?

—Yes. That's something else you didn't know about me.

-When did you discover this?

—When I was five. I got my first watch. A Hop-a-Long Cassidy Timex. I could hear it ticking in my right ear but not my left. I told my mum there was something wrong with the watch. And she rushed me to the ear, nose and throat clinic where they pronounced me deaf as a doorpost. Left is deaf. Right is all right.

—That's so sweet, Phillip. And sad.

I kissed Susan gently on the forehead.

—I've learned to live with it. I make sure people stand or

sit to my right when they're talking to me. My grandmother was deaf in the same ear. She'd say: If you want to borrow money, stand on my left. If you want to give me money, stand on my right.

Susan smiled.

—I have trouble hearing anyone who comes up from behind, Susan. But otherwise, it's okay. Let me carry on.

I finished my call but didn't turn the CD back on. As I reached up to a cupboard to put away some things, I heard music. I walked back over to the CD player. It was still turned off but there was music playing. I pulled the plug from the wall and the music didn't stop. Then I started hearing songs by artists and bands whose CD's I didn't even have. Continuous music. You know, like one of those 24-hour radio stations:

—KZ one-oh-nine. All music. All the time

A musical version of "voices in the head."

There was a coat on the back of a door in the hallway. When I glanced at it, I thought a man was standing there. I took a step forward to talk to him and he turned back into a coat.

I thought I heard people walking up and down the staircase.

I was hallucinating. Really, really badly.

I must have called an ambulance. I was suddenly outside sitting on the garden bench, but I don't remember leaving the house. A policeman arrived first and told me the paramedics were on the way. Then he asked something stupid like:

—Are you okay?

—No, I'm not actually, I said.

—Are you experiencing any pains?

—Not so much pains but noises and visions.

-Like what?

—CDs that play when the player is unplugged. Hanging coats that transform themselves in men. People who aren't there walking up and the stairs.

—I see, said the policeman.

—I don't think you do, mate, I replied.

Susan laughed out loud at that. I smiled and continued.

—I spent four day in the hospital on Librium and three weeks at

the Four Oaks Rehab Center. I went back home. I stayed sober for thirty days. And then I relapsed again. Jennifer flew back out from L.A. She saved my life.

—Phillip. I had no idea. I would never have known. You said you didn't drink and I didn't think any more of it. Wow, Phillip.

—Now you know. You had also asked about me being religious. Part of getting sober is putting your trust in a Higher Power. Having total faith that things will always work out.

Susan looked down at her hands. She raised one to my face and stroked my chin.

—Now I understand. Is this it then, Phillip? No more?

—Well, it's one day at a time as we say in AA. I heard once that some alcoholics have at least two or three relapses before getting truly sober. If that's the case, I hope I've had mine.

—Did you have blackouts or anything?

—Oh yes. People would tell me things I had done or places I had been, and I had no idea what they were talking about. Complete amnesia. Blackouts are really scary.

—Oh, Phillip.

—My AA sponsor would kill me if he knew about you. Alcoholics are not supposed to be involved in *any* relationship for at least a year after getting sober. Certainly not with a married person. We're supposed to protect ourselves against that kind of stress.

Susan sat up and kissed me on the lips. She ran her fingers down my back, scratching me lightly.

—No stress, Phillip. Just lovemaking. And fun.

—Dig your nails in. That's fun.

—Really?

—Yes. It turns me on. That's something else you didn't know about me. Scratch me really hard.

I handed her a tortoiseshell comb that was sitting on the bedside table. She examined it and shook her head to indicate that a comb wasn't good enough.

—We need something harder. And we have the perfect thing. Or even, a *pair* of things.

Jennifer

I hung up the phone after finally getting hold of Phillip. I knew when he was drinking and I was pretty certain that he was telling me the truth. He was staying sober. And he did seem happy actually. A relationship with a married woman wasn't the best thing for someone in recovery though. This much I knew from going to Al Anon—counseling for the families of alcoholics and addicts.

I plopped down on the sofa in my office.

When Phillip came to America in the early eighties, it seemed only natural I would follow.

He was only supposed to be here for six months but he fell in love. Always falling in love. He stayed, married Lauren, the kids came along. He established a good career here.

At the same time, all the English advertising commercials directors were being snapped up by Hollywood. British directors were suddenly in vogue in Tinseltown and this new wave of talent made movies like *Chariots of Fire, Alien, Flashdance, Fame,* and *Top Gun.*

The timing was perfect for me. I was working at Mott Productions in London and my boss, Ronnie Mott, got his first feature. We packed up and suddenly—here I was! And it's here I've stayed.

The irony wasn't lost on either of us that had I remained in London, I would still be the same distance from Phillip as I was in L.A. Somehow it seemed closer though. The same country, easier to reach each other if we needed to.

I drifted back to our childhood. Phillip and I were inseparable. A connection that wasn't quite normal. Mum told me Phillip fell off his bike once and hurt himself, but it was me that cried from the imagined pain. It really was a bit like that. Twins. Together. Always. We even shared a bed until we were eleven or twelve. It was only when the bed started shaking in the middle of the night and Phillip's left hand was exploring himself under the covers that I asked mum about single beds, like my friends had.

My first real kiss was with Phillip. Under the mistletoe one Christmas. No one seemed to be taking any notice and so we kept kissing until Auntie Dolly needed to get through the doorway.

—Out of the way, lovebirds, was all she said. It felt totally natural. And nice. When I had my first date, I asked Phillip how far I should let a boy go.

—A bit upstairs on the outside, he said. —And nothing downstairs.

Phillip's was the first erect cock I had ever seen. He hadn't locked the bathroom door and I accidentally burst in. I needed to pee. The bathroom was like a sauna. Phillip was just relaxing in the tub, enjoying the steam. His hard penis breaking the surface of the water.

—Oh, sorry. Can I use the loo?

—Of course.

I hoisted my skirt over my slender thighs and gathered it around my waist. I exposed white, schoolgirl-like knickers. No stockings. Phillip was watching me. I put my thumbs under the waistband and eased my knickers down slowly. I knew I was being provocative. I didn't care. Phillip didn't seem to mind either. My knickers came down over my knees. I sat down on the toilet, leaned forward and folded my hands in my lap. I glanced slowly at Phillip and smiled coyly. I peed, stood up, and flushed. I turned and faced the bath and slowly pulled my knickers up. I let my skirt fall down gradually over my thighs. I stepped forward, dipped one hand in the hot bath water and looked Phillip directly in the eyes. I shook my hand as if to wash it. And then I gently stroked his cock. Once. Just once. Very slowly. Very lightly. Using the very tips of my fingers. I kissed him on the forehead.

—Goodbye, darling brother.

The phone rang. Back to business. I was late for a meeting with Ronnie. I jumped up and ran out of the office.

Sarah

Naturally, I knew what was going on. When Susan asked me to take care of the shop for a few days because she was going away, it was obvious she wasn't planning a solo trip to a mountain retreat for purposes of spiritual enlightenment.

This would be more about refreshing the body than the mind.

I actually liked Phillip. I saw a lot of him now. In and out of the shop to pick up the latest piece for his collection.

—It's amazing where she finds these pieces, week after week, he had said somewhat naively.

Naturally, I was privy to the fact that there was a year's worth of such pieces locked away in the safe and that Susan was releasing pieces to Phillip one or two at a time to keep him coming back for more. For more of a lot of things, I would say.

Oh, the power of a collection. The power of a beautiful woman.

And she was still beautiful, after all these years.

I also realized why Phillip dropped into the shop when he knew Susan wouldn't be here. A little game, perhaps, to make it look like his visits to *Remains To Be Seen* weren't all Susan-centric, as it were.

Ah. Cunning stuff. But not much gets past Sarah. Not even at this advanced age.

Susan. Susan. Susan.

Susan had insisted Phillip was just a new friend. Well you don't fuck your friends. And I'm pretty certain Susan would sleep with Phillip. If she hadn't already.

I met Susan when we were in the ad business in London in the seventies.

I hired her actually. I was desperate for the help. One of

the problems with assembling a department composed largely of women was that the straight ones got married followed by getting pregnant. And then they were off. Back then, they rarely returned to the workplace but pursued suburban careers as good wives and mothers. It was worth the carousel effect this had on staffing though, just to be surrounded by these delicious young ladies. *Those were the days, my friend.*

I remember looking over Susan's resume, calling Bardell & Associates, the headhunters, and asking Patsy Bardell to send her over.

—She's gorgeous, said Patsy.

I ignored the sexually charged comment.

—Yes, Patsy, but is she as good as her resume?

—She's gorgeous.

—Have her call.

It was rumored that Patsy had sex of one sort or another with all of her candidates and her agency clients. She had a nickname: advertising's casting couch. Or as one wag put it, you just lay on her, push her pillows around a bit, and get comfy.

Whether it was true or not, it seemed to be working.

Her candidates always got the best jobs. Her clients got the best candidates. And Patsy got laid. Along with a fifteen percent commission on the candidate's first year's salary.

Nice work if you can get it.

Susan wanted to come in at the end of the day. It would be easier than cutting out of work during office hours. It was 6:00 sharp when my phone rang. The receptionist had gone for the day and Susan called from the lobby using the nighttime directory the receptionist always left on her desk.

—I'll be right down, I told her.

I looked in the mirror hanging on the back of my office door. Short hair. Roundish face. Pretty, I thought. Half-closed eyes. English. Very English. I ran my hand through my hair. Touched up my lipstick. I wasn't one of those no make-up lesbians. I was a girl who just happened to like girls. Nothing wrong with that.

Susan was sitting on the black leather sofa with chrome arms you've seen in a million reception areas. She was wearing a short, grey plaid skirt. Lovely. She had on a tight cashmere sweater that I immediately wanted to run my hands over.

She stood up.

–Sarah?

–Yes, Susan. Welcome to MKT Advertising. It's rather quiet. Most people have gone for the day. Or they're round the pub. Let's go to my office and then maybe a quick drink ourselves if you'd like.

–That sounds good, Sarah.

I liked the way she said my name at the end of the sentence. Something I would come to love over the years.

We got into the elevator and she turned to me, looking at me carefully. Not shy at all.

–You look like that English actress.

I had been told that before. I knew exactly the actress she meant.

–It must be the hair.

She laughed.

–Not just that. You're pretty like her, Sarah.

–Okay, you've got the job. I love brown-noses. Let me get my bag and we'll go round the pub.

And that was it. I was in love. The start of a life-long friendship. The sex started just a few months after Susan came to work for me; just days after she got back from her honeymoon actually. It was late again. I thought everyone had left the office.

–Knock, knock.

I looked up. Susan was rapping an imaginary door with her closed fist. I put down the media plan I was reading.

–Come in. I didn't realize people were still here.

–Yes. Just me though, Sarah. Everyone else went round the pub. I was waiting for James but he's stood me up. Working late.

She hesitated in the doorway. I pushed back my chair, leaned over to a cabinet at the side of the desk and pulled a bottle of vodka out of the bottom drawer. I held it up and wiggled it.

—Drink?

—Mmm, that would be nice.

Susan stepped into the office and went to the little refrigerator tucked discreetly in the corner next to the sofa. She picked up the tumblers that were sitting on top of it with one hand and opened the fridge door with the other. She grabbed a bottle of tonic water. I took a good look at her as she brought everything over to my desk.

She was wearing a pretty summer dress. A sort of 1940s style. Small flowers on a pastel background. White buttons up the front; fitted around her breasts; flowing around her thighs. She had on high heels. I could see a painted nail peeping through the open toe. She put down the tumblers and tonic. I had the vodka in my left hand. I patted the right side of the desktop with my free hand. Susan didn't take her eyes off me. She came around the desk and leaned against the spot I had touched. Her legs parted ever so slightly as she pushed back and sat on the desk. The soft fabric of her dress fell in folds between her thighs. She swung her right foot like a pendulum until her shoe loosened and came off. I poured the drinks and handed her one.

—Cheers, she said, her eyes searching my face.

—Cheers! You really haven't talked much about your honeymoon. Did you have a nice time?

Susan looked down at her glass and then straight at me.

—I thought about you a lot.

I opened my eyes wide and raised my eyebrows as if to say, *Really?* Susan continued.

—About our kiss. Outside Kettner's.

I put down my glass and swiveled round on my chair towards her. I lifted her bare foot into my lap. The very tips of my fingers dusting her toes lightly.

—And...

—Well, I obviously thought that maybe I should have been concentrating on my new husband.

I laughed. She smiled. She was beautiful. I let my hand glide up her calf. She let her head fall back. She closed her eyes. Slowly. Her lips parted. I heard the softest moan. I let my hand continue up. It was now between her thighs. They were cold and smooth to the touch. She put down her drink and angled herself more towards me. I heard her other shoe fall to the floor and felt her wiggling toes as she put her left foot into my lap. She parted her knees and placed her hands on her dress. She pulled it up, ever so slowly.

—You've only been married a few days, Susan.

—Does making love to a woman count as being unfaithful?

I laughed. —Some husbands might quite like the idea.

She shifted her feet off my lap and placed them on the floor either side of my chair. As she lifted her dress higher still, I saw she had the skimpiest of panties on. Barely covering her young, slender thighs. She sat down on me. I felt her squeezing her buttocks in order to push deeper into my lap. Her hands went around my neck. I looked up and tickled her lips with mine. I unbuttoned the front of her dress. No bra. She was obviously dressed to be undressed. For James? Had he really stood her up? Maybe not. I didn't care. Not that night. Nor any of the other days and nights to come that we would make love.

I always knew she would never desert her new husband for me. James was someone that she would be with all her life. She would live her straight life with James and add an occasional twist to keep things interesting. I would learn over the years Susan always got what she wanted. Enjoyed it. And moved on.

I never moved on. After she left for the States, I went into a severe depression. I hankered after her. Getting the job in the New York office of MKT was totally engineered to enable me to be closer to her. Simple as that. At the time, as with so many life experiences, I had no way of knowing where all this would lead.

I certainly wouldn't have predicted that I would be sitting here in upstate New York, minding the shop figuratively and literally, while Susan was off getting seen to by her male lover. Minding the shop and knowing exactly what to say and how to cover up should James drop by unexpectedly.

I would do anything for Susan.

One must live in hope.

Susan

I looked at the grandfather clock standing proudly in the corner of the shop. It was two minutes to five. I always closed bang on time unless there was a lingering customer who looked like they really *were* going to make a decision between the silver Georgian teapot and the turn of the century Denby platter.

Tonight, there were no such customers.

Everything was arranged with Sarah. She would watch the shop. And she'd watch my back. It was unspoken but I believed she knew what I was up to. I also knew she would cover for me should anything come up with James.

Oh, Sarah.

I had thought about her non-stop during my honeymoon. They say every woman will fantasize occasionally about another man while they're making love to their partner. But I was truly imagining Sarah. I made James kiss me really lightly so I could pretend his lips were Sarah's.

The first night Sarah and I made love was exquisite. I stayed late at the office because I wanted her. I had watched her all day as she went about her work. Leaning over the other girls' desks. When she looked or smiled at me, I felt myself getting wet. I had to have her.

We left the door to Sarah's office open. She had turned off her desk lamp. The only light in the room was coming from the corridor outside. It was dangerous and exciting. After she had undressed me, she sat me on the edge of her desk. I was facing my reflection in the window. I didn't recognize myself. It was like watching a movie. My arms were stretched out either side of my body, palms flat on the desk. I could just make out the shadowy image of my breasts. My legs were open, over Sarah's bare shoulders. I could see her naked back reflected in the glass. The back of her head going up and down in my lap. I could feel her warm tongue. First inside my vagina, then lightly up and down over my clitoris making it swell and contract. She expertly closed her lips around it, forcing it to grow again. I came in waves. Sarah stood to her feet and kissed me deeply. I could taste myself on her tongue and lips. Her breasts pushed into mine. A feeling that could never exist between a man and a woman. I wanted to tell her I loved her. Right at that moment, all those years ago, I wanted nothing but her.

But now I was suddenly aware of the clock ticking. Tick. Tick. Tick. The ornate minute hand finally jumped to 4:59.

–Bugger it.

A couple was coming up the path. I leapt up, banging my knee on the corner of the desk in my rush, and raced to the door.

I twisted the sign around, banging it against the window so they would definitely hear me and see it.

There. *Closed.*

The startled couple stared at me as if I had two heads. They turned around and walked quickly in the direction they had come.

On the way back to my desk, I glanced at myself in one of the many old mirrors that lined the wall.

James was on his way out of town.

I stared hard at myself.

And Phillip was on his way here from the city.

His train was getting into nearby Woodford station at 5:07.

A short cab ride. And he'd be here by 5:15. At the very

latest. My stomach was doing flip-flops.

Phillip

We'd known each other for more than two months by this time. We'd already been lovers. But we'd never actually contrived a situation where we'd meet while her husband was out of town.

Sneaking a few hours at my house was one thing.

But this was different.

A friend of mine had a house in Newport I could use anytime. I had taken the kids there last summer. But apart from that, I'd never taken advantage of it.

Susan had strongly encouraged James to go on a golf trip to Florida his club had organized, when in actual fact, he really was undecided whether he wanted to go.

We were going to have three days together. Something we'd never done before. A naughty weekend.

And Sarah was going to look after the shop.

I stood up and grabbed my weekend bag from the overhead rack as the train pulled into the station. I was just a few minutes away from her.

Susan

The moment he walked into the shop that evening, I knew we wouldn't be leaving for Newport without making love first. He smiled his smile. He was wearing a black blazer, unbuttoned. It draped in a way that I can only describe as sensual. His blue striped shirt looked as fresh as if he'd just put it on. His cuffed pants broke perfectly over a pair of loafers. I loved the way he looked. I locked the door behind him and took the initiative.

I pushed my tongue deep into his mouth. I reached inside his jacket, sliding my hands around his back and tugging at his shirt until it came free from the waistband of his trousers. I slipped my hand up the inside his shirt, fingering my way up his spine. It made him shiver. He arched his back. I could feel him, hard against my lower stomach.

I felt my dress come apart at the back as he pulled the zipper down slowly as far as it would go. The dress fell to the floor. I stepped out of my shoes. I was wearing a full-length slip. Nothing else. My nipples were hard, the silk of the slip outlining them clearly. So sensitive, they almost hurt. I closed my eyes as I felt one of his hands go around my waist while the other inched inside my slip and up the back of my thighs. Cold and soft. Now his hand was over my buttocks. Massaging. Stroking. Ever so gently pinching. I reached down and undid his fly. I worked my hand inside the tight space between us. Down over the top of his briefs until I felt him. I cupped my hand around him. Working up and down. I let my head fall back and to one side, letting out a small breath. Soft and faint. I momentarily opened my eyes. Through the doorway, I saw the Edwardian sofa in the adjoining room.

Phillip

After we made love in the shop, Susan got dressed and I put on jeans and a T-shirt from my bag. We slipped through the basement and out into the customer parking spaces where Susan had parked the Range Rover. I had been in Manhattan all day and had deliberately left my car at home, in the driveway where it would be seen. J.C. was spending the weekend at my dog-sitter's house. I was free to be with Susan. Although free was a relative term. I had found myself wanting her more and more despite all my good intentions that this was just to be an affair. Nothing more. But I was falling for her. I wanted to rescue her from an unhappy marriage. Well, a boring one anyway.

I started having visions of us being together long term.

I was planning a future my heart wanted but my head knew was impossible while Susan was still with James. And she had never indicated for one moment that leaving James was in the cards. Sure, she complained about him. She said she was disappointed not to have more love in the marriage. She facetiously said he wore his best pajamas in bed to turn her on. She wanted some fun and excitement before she *popped her clogs* as she put it—an English expression for taking off your shoes one last time before you die.

She said all those things but she never said she would walk out on her husband. Not yet anyway.

I threw our bags on the back seat. Susan would drive until we got to Connecticut. If anyone saw us, she was simply driving a customer home. I would take over once we hit the interstate. Then, as promised, I would drive her to Newport and drive her wild.

We had taken our time making love in the shop—we were in no hurry—and the delay worked in our favor. By the time we got on the road, the evening rush-hour traffic had died down. We made the interstate quickly and I took over the wheel.

—I brought some CDs, I told her. —They're in the outside pocket of my bag.

Susan slipped off her seat belt, turned around, and leaned through the space between the front seats reaching for the CDs. Her arse was right by my right hand. I slapped her gently.

—You've got a great arse, Susan.

She stopped reaching for my bag and looked at me.

—You know, I do actually. I was moisturizing it the other day in front of the mirror, and that was exactly what I said to myself. You've got a great arse, Susan.

—Ah, modesty prevails.

—Hey, listen mate. I could have been covered in a Burka all these years as far as James was concerned. I like the fact I'm enjoying my body.

—And that it's being enjoyed by me.

—That's right, Phillip. That you're enjoying it too.

She got the CDs but not before I slapped her gently

again.

—Ah, you've got all the greats. Who do you want to listen to, Phillip? Sarah McLachlan? Bonnie Raitt? Willie Nelson? I hear a bit of Willie is always good.

—You would know, my dear.

Susan slipped in a CD. As the soulful music started playing, I felt her looking me over carefully. She shook her head slightly.

—You're a romantic, aren't you, Phillip?

—Am I? I suppose I am in a way. I didn't think I needed to be in a relationship but I'm enjoying this. Whatever this is. And I like to listen to good old blubbery music and have candlelit dinners, letting my love melt like chocolate…

—Oh stop it. That's horrible.

—By the way, I brought some romance novels for us to read in bed. Barbara Cartland, Anne Mallory—

—You did not!

I laughed out loud.

—Susan! I'm winding you up.

The journey zipped by. We were just a few minutes away from the bridge that would take us over Narragansett Bay to Newport. It was quite dark now and the bridge was ablaze with twinkling lights. It was really pretty.

—At the risk of being called a romantic again, isn't that beautiful, Susan?

—Yes, Phillip. It is. But I can't wait to slide into bed with you. I want SEX!

She shouted the last word.

I laughed with her.

But it seemed our passion might be leading down different paths.

Love and romance? Or simply lust and sex?

Susan

It was a bit risky coming to Newport in a way. Although the only person who knew we'd be here was Phillip's pal, owner of the house we were using for our naughty weekend. Phillip hadn't even told *him* any details. I was just a friend.

It was a little over a two-hour drive. Even leaving the shop at 6:30 still put us in the center of town before 9:00. And there wasn't the fuss of a ferry. As beautiful as Block Island to the south of Newport is, getting on and off the ferry was sometimes a pain.

Newport was easier all round. The risk of us being seen by someone we knew was, as Phillip put it, somewhat diminished given this was the end of February—hardly the height of the season—and by our resolve to climb into bed and not get out until it was time to leave.

We were fully expecting most places to be shut up tight still after the winter but on Thames Street—the main drag—the lights were blazing and people were coming in and out of bars and restaurants.

The only difference between now and July was the fact everyone was bundled up instead of being scantily clad in shorts, T-shirts, and open-toe sandals.

Phillip knew Newport quite well. Other friends of his sailed from up here. Phillip told me he even took part in the annual Newport to Bermuda Yacht Race one year, but being a deckhand and eating reheated food followed by losing it over the side a few minutes later wasn't his idea of fun.

Phillip slowed down in front of a three-story, colonial-era building—typical of those you find in New England seaport towns. It was probably an inn once but now housed a French restaurant on the ground floor.

—Do you want to eat here? It's too late to go food shopping.

—Whatever you want to do. If we are seen, so be it.

—I think we'll be fine, Susan.

Phillip parked a little way down the street and we walked back along the uneven pavement, victim of the thousands of tourists who pounded it during the season.

The restaurant door opened into a small vestibule. A very pretty girl stood behind a mahogany lectern. Big red lips. Sparkling eyes. Long, blonde hair. She stepped around the lectern to reveal that she was wearing a short, black skirt. She was lovely. That little part of me, my sapphic side, tingled. To the left was a warm, inviting bar, partially hidden by long, burgundy velvet drapes. Very French. The dining room was to the right. A largish room, but with a low ceiling which kept the cozy feeling. There were probably a dozen or so tables. People seated at about half of them. Clean white tablecloths. Brass lamps on each table with silk shades. At the end of the room was a dark oak dresser. It was crowned with one large mirror and a series of smaller ones. Twisted columns of oak held up small shelves that in turn held votive candles whose flames danced in mirrored reflections.

Chopin's *Raindrop* was playing. It was perfect.

My new blonde friend showed us the way. I pulled on Phillip's arm and held him back momentarily to let her get a few steps ahead of us. She was wearing three-inch heels. I looked up and down her long, luscious legs. I felt a little twinge in my minge. Phillip whispered in my ear.

–Let's ask her back after dinner.

–I'm up for it, I said without hesitation.

He looked at me. Maybe that wasn't what he was expecting to hear but he seemed to delight in it. A big smile came over his face as blondie stopped at our table. I let my hand lightly touch hers as she handed us menus. She smiled at me. That twinge again.

–What's your name?

–Amanda.

–Well, I'm Phillip. And this is Susan.

Where was Phillip going with this?

–You're very beautiful, Amanda.

Holy crap, Phillip, I thought. You're not going to actually do it, are you? Ask her back? Let's at least order first!

–Isn't she beautiful, Susan?

I was outrageously wet between the legs. Not damp. Not moist. Wet. I could barely get the words out but I did. I even managed to purr.

—Yes, Amanda. You're very beautiful.

Amanda smiled at Phillip but let her gaze linger on me. And I don't think I was imagining it.

—Thank you. Very much. I'll be back to take your order. Let me know if you have any questions.

Any questions? I could only imagine what Phillip was thinking. —Here's a question, Amanda. Have you ever fucked three ways?

She turned and walked away. One foot very carefully in front of the other. A way of walking favored by models to make their hips and shoulders swing with maximum sexuality. Oh, our Amanda knew what she was doing all right.

Phillip would be playing the old clit lip trick again for me tonight. Just like he did in the *Ha-Ha* cupboard. But now I could put a face to pussy. I needed to look at the menu. Concentrate on eating *food* first. Phillip put his hand over mine.

—Susan, I've left my glasses in the car. Will you read the menu to me?

—Of course, Phillip. *Assurément.*

I put on my best Sarah Bernhardt murmur followed by a sultry English translation. I let the words drip out.

—*Napoléon d'Aubergine, Tomate et Fromage.* Layers of Marinated Eggplant, Tomato & Mozzarella. *Carpaccio de Filet Mignon au Huile de Truffe.* Sliced Carpaccio of Beef, garnished with Arugula, Caper Berries, and Truffle Oil.

I looked up to make sure Phillip was listening and then went back at the menu.

—*Mélange des Pussy.*

—I'm sorry, Susan?

—Oops, my mistake, Phillip. I meant *Melange de Poisson!* I blew him a kiss.

—There's also *Magret de Canard au Café.* Duck breast sautéed with a Coffee Crust.

—I fancy a duck.

—You would, Phillip.

—Well, you had your eye on the *mélange de pussy*.

—Talking of pussy, here comes Amanda now. No joking around while we order.

Sarah

James called about 9:30. He had been trying to reach Susan to let her know he had arrived safely in Florida but kept getting her voicemail. Had I seen her this evening? Were the lights on over at the main house? I told him I had not seen her tonight but I *could* see some lights burning at the house. Maybe she was out at dinner. I didn't actually lie. But I knew for certain I had lied by omission. I didn't feel good about that. Not at all.

Susan

Amanda sashayed over carrying two flutes of champagne but no notepad to take our order.

—These are from a gentleman at the bar. He says *salute* and *bon appetite*.

My mood changed. Shit. Someone's seen us. Someone right here in the fucking restaurant. I was suddenly inexplicably angry with Phillip for bringing us here. Phillip was very calm.

—There must be a mistake. No one we know would know we're here.

I could hear Amanda's brain whirring as she processed that one.

—Sir, I think he just wanted to toast you. He said something about admiring people in love and how they deserved the finest champagne. Shall I take it back?

Phillip started to say yes and I cut in.

—No, no, please. We accept.

Hey, champagne is champagne. And since Phillip wouldn't drink his, I'd make sure it didn't go to waste. As I used to say in Kettner's, give me a flute and I'll wet my whistle.

—You can leave both glasses, Amanda. Thank you. Please express our thanks to the kind gentleman. And we're ready to order. I'm ravenous.

—*Ravishing.*

Phillip, Amanda, and I all looked up at once. I assumed this was the gentleman from the bar. Old Champagne Charlie. He spoke with a soft French accent. He was very handsome and had obviously worked his charm many times before. He knew his way around the seduction block.

—You're *ravishing*, Madam.

A roll of the *rrr's* on ravishing. He turned to Phillip.

—May I compliment you on your wife, sir?

Phillip smiled.

—You may indeed.

Phillip being my husband didn't seem to compute for Amanda. I think she liked the earlier thought that we were secret lovers, here in Newport for a dirty weekend. Which was of course, the truth. Champagne Charlie raised his glass.

—I cannot bear to see lovers *sans* champagne. Life is too short. We must drink to love and passion always.

This bloke was bonkers. But the champagne looked jolly good.

I raised my glass, took a sip, and put it down.

Champagne Charlie kissed my hand.

Phillip merely pretended to raise the glass but left his champagne sitting firmly on the table.

—Enjoy your beautiful evening together. *Au revoir.*

He turned to Amanda, winked seductively at her, and then he was gone. Amanda turned to us.

—I'll be right back to take your order.

Phillip

The food was delicious. I ended up having the special. *Carré D'Agneau, Sauce Fine Herbes*—Rack of Lamb, roasted with herbs.

Susan stayed with her choice of *foie gras* and a second appetizer as her main course, *mélange de Poisson*.

The meal came and went.

—Shall we get the bill? I'm ready for bed.

—Of course, Susan. I'm not sure Amanda is up for coming with us though.

The restaurant was empty now. Amanda was leaning against the back wall, chatting with a waitress. She had slipped one foot out of her shoe and was rubbing her toes on the back of her other lovely leg. It was very sexy. But she was done for the day. You could see that. She wanted to go home. We paid the bill and went out to the street.

—Kiss me gently, Susan said. —Pretend you're Amanda.

I let my lips glide over hers. Until they tingled.

—I'll find a way to get Amanda into bed with us later, Susan.

—Maybe she'll join us for dessert.

Susan was already beginning to love my little bedtime stories. Already figuring out plots for me to embellish. She told me just the sound of me whispering to her made her wet. She almost didn't need the story.

—Dessert? I said lowering my voice. —I think I know a story about dessert. Strawberries and lots and lots of cream.

She let out a little moan.

A Feast of You.

My appetizer
And main course.
My salad
And dessert.
My soup,
My snack,
No food I lack,
Not even
Blue *Roquefort.*
The main menu,
And tasty stew,
Your perfume
Sweet as dill.
Such nourishment
You are to me—
I'm careful
Not to spill.
I eat you up
With relish.
I can never
Get enough.
Your body is
The perfect dish.
My Fav-or-ite
Food stuff.

Susan

Phillip's friend's place was charming. It was an old carriage house—ours for the asking anytime at all.

I could get used to this little love nest. We dropped our bags on the bedroom floor. Phillip went to put mine on the bed, looked at me, looked at the inviting bed, and decided to leave the bag where it was. I stripped off and wandered into the bathroom.

—Have you seen this, Phillip? A double shower?

I hadn't realized that he was standing right behind me. Naked.

Phillip

Susan came out of the bathroom wearing nothing but a smile. We had just made love under hot running water. She had stayed in the shower to wash her hair. Now she had a freshly scrubbed glow and that lovely clean smell. She walked towards the bed where I was stretched out, reading an old *New Yorker*. She was carrying a slightly limp towel in one hand and a hairbrush in the other. An English Mason Pearson. She threw the towel down on the bed and started brushing her wet hair back. She walked very lightly on her toes around the room not wanting to get the bottoms of her newly-bathed feet dirty. It was kind of sexy. She turned to her bag on the floor and pulled out a silk nightie.

—You don't need that.

She immediately threw it down and turned back to me.

Her pubic hairs were still damp from the shower and this

gave them the appearance of being darker and fuller.

–Do you ever bikini wax?

–I used to, Phillip. I haven't paid much attention in that department in recent years. I could shave it all off and James would never notice.

–Well, let's give it a go and see. Maybe not all of it. But a nice short back and sides, as my dad's barber would say. Come over here.

Susan

Phillip got up and grabbed the towel. He smoothed it out flat on the bed.

–Lay down. Across the bed. Dangle your feet over the side.

I did as I was told.

–I'll be right back.

I heard water running in the bathroom and then the faucet being shut off.

Phillip reappeared holding his razor, a can of shaving foam, and a steaming facecloth. He put them all down on the edge of the towel next to me and retrieved his glasses from the bedside table.

He put them on with a certain deliberation, like a surgeon putting on his gloves before an operation.

–Right, he said firmly.

I felt the delicious warmth of the facecloth as he pushed it in circular motions around my pubes. Then there was that aerosol squish sound as a good dollop of shaving foam squirted free from the can.

–Close your eyes. You'll enjoy this.

–I'm a bit nervous. There's a certain gynecological thing going on here.

Phillip laughed. He got down on his knees and spread my legs carefully. He scooted up between them, adjusted his glasses and went in.

–Don't worry. I'm good at this. I shave every day.

–Not pussy, you don't. Well, I presume you don't.

–You'll love it, Susan.

And I did. The cream was cold and startling after the warmth of the facecloth.

Then the sensation of warm steel as the razor did its work on the old female forest. Phillip went back to the bathroom to rinse off the razor with very hot water and there was a slight shock each time as the freshly washed blade made contact with my skin. I felt the warm cloth again as he wiped away loose hairs and dabbed up the foam the razor hadn't cleaned away.

His hand felt very soft and gentle as it made contact with skin that hadn't seen the light of day since I was a teenager.

–Wow. You look like a fresh young virgin, Susan. Stand up. Don't look yet.

Phillip put his hand over my eyes as he helped me up.

–Now look.

He took away his hand. I was facing the full-length mirror on the closet door. I gasped.

–Oh my, Phillip. I'm bald.

–Do you love it?

–It's beautiful. Is this what all the young girls do today?

He smiled with an innocent *I guess so* look on his face. I stood with my legs slightly apart, hands on hips. Phillip was standing behind me, looking over my shoulder at my reflection. He had created a perfect horizon line just above where my legs joined my groin.

Gone was the thick bush that had spread across my lower hemisphere over the years. He had thinned out all the remaining hair. I could see my clitoris. I let my hand wander down over the newly revealed skin. It was supremely smooth.

–That razor works wonders, Phillip.

Phillip put on a TV announcer's voice.

–*Two blades. The first one shaves you close. The second, closer still.*

He reached around and put his hand over mine and we massaged the smooth spot together.

I felt him go hard behind me. I turned around, pressed up against him, wiggled, and took his face in my hands.

–Thank you, darling, I whispered. –It's really beautiful.

Phillip

The rest of the weekend went pretty much as scheduled. We spent an inordinate amount of time in bed. Like John and Yoko's famous bed-in at the Amsterdam Hilton in 1969. Except we didn't use the occasion to protest the war in Vietnam or anywhere else. We simply made love. We got up to eat. Made a fire. Made love again. And slept. We had never spent overnight together. It was very special. Waking up in each other's arms. Drifting in and out of sleep and lovemaking. Never quite sure if we were actually awake or not. A dream. With occasional fantasy visits from the delicious Amanda. In our little made-up stories we ordered takeout from the restaurant, which naturally, Amanda delivered. We invited her in and she stayed. Sliding out of her clothes and into bed next to Susan while I watched. Amanda likes what I like, I whispered in Susan's ear. And Susan would come just at the thought of it.

In the middle of our last night in Newport, Susan rolled over and stroked my face.

–I never want this to end, Phillip.

My heart leapt. Neither did I.

Susan

Early to bed, early to rise! I was delighted to discover Phillip was one of those men who got up before they get up in the morning.

I didn't let it go to waste.

One morning I reached across and gently stroked his hard cock until he opened his eyes. The next morning I slipped under the covers, climbed over him, and worked my way up his body until I was sitting astride him.

He was sleeping, his cock wasn't. I lowered myself onto his fully erect manhood.

He was so hard I wondered whether there was any blood left in the rest of him.

He didn't say anything but seemed to be in a dream. A small smile on his beautiful lips.

We had this connection—a sexual rapport—even when he was barely awake.

An Ecstasy of Connection.

The phone rings
And I know it's you.
You think a thought
And I do too.
Each waking moment
You're on my mind.
This is a love
Of a different kind.
Emotional bonds
And mutual liking.
Sharing trust
And tears and crying.
We once crossed paths
And crossed again.
But this time round
We said Amen.
A lifetime searching
For the missing part.
The puzzle piece
That completes our heart.
They talk of chemistry,
But we have more,
An Ecstasy of Connection,
A Heavenly Rapport.

Does Susan really feel the way I feel?
She said she never wanted it to end.

Susan

It had been raining hard since I opened the shop at 11:00. The few people who did come in made no pretense about the fact they were only there to shelter from the downpour. I could hear the drip, drip, drip of rain in the *Ha-Ha* cupboard. I must get that fixed. As the rain slowed to a trickle, so the people trickled out into the street again and I was left alone once more. The grandfather clock struck 1:00. I stepped to the door and turned the sign around to *Closed*, just as Phillip had done when he was here yesterday. I slid the heavy bolt across the door and slipped off my shoes—the high black heels he loved me to wear.

The area rug felt soft and sensual against the bottom of my feet. He liked to let his fingers touch my feet ever so lightly knowing how ticklish I was. And then he'd let his lovely hands wander up the inside of my calves, behind my knees, slowly between my thighs. Now I was sitting in the leather wingback chair by the window. We had escalated the level of danger to making love regularly in the shop with only a flimsy net curtain between us and the outside world. We didn't bother with the *Ha-Ha* cupboard anymore. The risk of being caught was exciting and while we were fucking in a frenzy, I simply didn't care. Now I lifted my skirt way up above my knees. The sun had come out and the dappled light through the window warmed my thighs.

I found myself thinking of his head resting between my legs. Yesterday, I had run my fingers through his beautiful hair. Now I let my fingers run up my legs. Slowly, effortlessly, caressing myself. I imagined him sliding his hands under my skirt, reaching for the waistband of my panties. I raised my hips and slid my panties down over my knees. I only got one foot out before I wanted myself. I threw my head back against the chair. Closed my eyes. I let my middle finger part my vagina. When I got wet, he called it velvety. I slowly let my finger caress up and down the lips until it got to my swollen clitoris. I moved my index finger in a circular motion, just as he did. I grouped my fingers together and pretended it was his tongue, warm and wet. I slid all four fingers inside myself. Hard. It almost hurt. I was very wet.

I pulled out my fingers and gasped. I put them straight in my mouth, sucking them, tasting myself. With the fingers of one hand still in my mouth, I put the other hand on my vagina. Pushing against myself. Still sucking on the body perfume remaining on my fingers. He loved to watch me do that. He said it was like I was making love to another woman. I massaged myself to a wonderful climax. I opened my eyes and took in a lungful of my own sweet air.

I wanted more.

Sarah

When I turned up at the shop at lunchtime, the *Closed* sign was on the door. I used my key but the door was bolted from the inside. I walked over to the window and squinted through the net curtain. I could just about see that Susan was sitting in the wingback chair. She had slid halfway down, her eyes were closed, her knees pushed out from the seat, and her legs open. I knocked gently on the window. She looked up and saw it was me. I walked back to the door. I heard the bolt being pulled back. Susan popped only her head out, as if hiding behind a bathroom door because she was naked.

–Am I interrupting something, Susan?
–No, Sarah. You've come at just the right time.

Phillip

Susan told me she needed to take care of the home front for a few days but then suddenly called me. She invited me to stop by—ostensibly—to pick up a FedEx that was being delivered to her house.

She had seen a pair of George Sangster silver serving spoons with Edinburgh hallmarks dating to 1850 at a fair a few weeks earlier. Susan thought I should have them and she had them shipped.

James was also at home apparently, but leaving shortly to attend a Yale Club get together with his old Wall Street chums.

I primed her over the phone and then drove to her house.

Susan

I had called Phillip to let him know I had found some new pieces for him. The business part of the call lasted about ten seconds and then we got down to monkey business. It was the first time we had phone sex. A dreadful turn of phrase but that's the only way to describe it. I was trying to tell him about the silver but then he started whispering to me.

—Where are you?

—In my bedroom.

—Is James home?

—Yes.

—Even better.

—What are you talking about, Phillip?

—What are you wearing?

—The black dress you like, I said.

I wasn't—it was an old green dress—but I had a feeling I knew where this was going.

—Walk over to the mirror.

—I'm already here.

–Are you looking at yourself?

–Yes.

–The dress has a zip down the back, right?

–Yes.

–Can you reach around with one hand?

–Yes, I can.

–Imagine I'm unzipping you.

–Phillip! What if James comes up?

–So what? You're simply getting undressed.

Phillip paused, lowered his whisper even more, and corrected himself. –*Being* undressed. By your lover.

That was it.

Knowing James was downstairs, knowing that Phillip was about to undress me, I almost came from that alone.

I pulled the zip down slowly and sensually, dropping my shoulders one at a time until I could wriggle free of the dress without putting down the phone.

–Take down your panties, Susan. Slowly.

I put my thumb and forefinger inside the waistband and awkwardly pushed my knickers down over my hips, over my arse, over my thighs and knees, and shook them free from my ankles.

–Now your bra, he commanded. –But don't take it off. Just let your shoulder straps fall over your arms.

–Oh…

–Can you see the reflection of your bed in the mirror?

–Yes…yes…

I could barely get that one word out.

–Imagine me on it. I am hard. I open my arms and ask you to come to me. *Come* with me.

I stepped towards the bed but I was already orgasming. I just rolled on to it.

–Where are you, Phillip?

–Naked, on my bed.

I didn't need any further instructions. My hand went straight to my clitoris. And I came in waves.

James

Susan had originally said she would drive me to the station. I had an afternoon's drinking in front of me at the Yale Club with old colleagues and I didn't want to be driving home after that. Then she said she couldn't leave the house because she was expecting FedEx and needed to sign for the delivery. So she called a cab for me. It turned up very early. She was in the bedroom. When I went up to say goodbye, the door was closed. I could hear that she was talking to someone on the phone. I waited for the call to end until I couldn't wait any longer.

Susan

I slipped on some jeans and a baggy shirt and went downstairs. James had already gone. The cab must have come early. I called him on his cell thirty minutes later to make sure he was on the train. Safely heading out before Phillip headed in. FedEx notified me that the package had been delayed because of a customs backlog but would definitely be delivered sometime that day.

We had promised never to make love in my house. Off-limits. Out of bounds. Forbidden Territory. Danger. Do not enter.

But then Phillip showed up. I was still hot from the phone sex. One look at each other and that was it.

I took his arm and pulled him through to the dining room. I slid my hands under his sweater, then under his shirt. I pulled them up together, gliding my fingers over his chest, down his back, along his spine until he shivered.

Ding Dong.

–An intervention, he laughed.

–Don't move, I commanded.

The simple act of signing for the FedEx and taking the package seemed to take hours. I practically slammed the door in the driver's face.

I put the FedEx box down on the hall table and went back into the dining room. Phillip's sweater and shirt were lying in a heap on the floor. I walked through to the kitchen. He wasn't there. I thought I heard a movement upstairs.

No, not in my bed. Not where James and I had slept for so many married years.

But Phillip was in the guest room. Stretched out naked. One knee up in the air. His hands behind his head. His eyes closed. Breathing slowly.

He heard me come into the room.

We said nothing. I slipped out of my jeans. Pulled my shirt over my head. Slid out of my panties. The gentle sound of me undressing stirred him.

I watched as his penis grew harder. I took him in my hands. Touched him the way he loved—one hand on his cock, the other, caressing his balls. He didn't move. Just opened his eyes and smiled. I climbed over him. I was already wet. I lowered myself and held on to his broad shoulders.

He pushed up from the bed and we rolled over. Now he was on top. Sliding all the way into me but then ever so slowly, withdrawing until the very tip of his cock was on the very outside of my vagina, almost losing contact.

Then he thrust back in hard.

Banging beautifully against me. Repeating this over and over until he cried out, until the air went out of him, and he collapsed his full weight on me.

I loved when he crumpled.

It signaled he was done.

Spent.

I whispered in his ear.

—Was that good, baby?

—Oh, yes. Wonderful. And you?

I took his face in my hands and looked him straight in the eyes.

—I don't know what you're doing to me, Phillip.

And I truly didn't.

Phillip

Susan said she didn't know what I was doing to her. But I knew exactly what she was doing to me. She was making me fall in love with her. And I couldn't help myself.

She was the one that usually started it. She got the ball rolling and my balls roiling. Take the afternoon *sur le table*. The table in the center of the shop.

When I arrived at *Remains*, the table had been cleared of everything except the intricate, ivory-colored damask runner that lay along its length. All the china and bric-a-brac that had formed the shop's eye-catching centerpiece now sat on the floor. I had never noticed what a beautiful table it was before. An oval drop-leaf. Center drawer. Polished mahogany—the color of a well-worn bar in an English country pub.

I peeked over the table and saw that Susan was on the floor, on her hands and knees. She was wrapping a delicate tea service and carefully putting the pieces into a box. Royal Albert Vintage, Bone China, 1920s, she had told me proudly several days ago. But now she was putting it away. I wondered why. Her doggy-crouch position showed off her full moon of an arse. I tried not to move. I didn't want to disturb the moment. She must have felt me staring at her and looked up over her left shoulder.

—Oh, hello. Enjoying the view?

—Indeed, darling. It looks lovely from here. What are you doing?

—Well, there were bits and pieces that weren't moving. So I'm putting them away for now and replacing them with some new things I had shipped over.

She looked around at the jumble on the floor. A smile crept over her face. She splayed out her elbows and dropped her shoulders. Her beautiful bottom was raised up several inches now, her back arched. She looked at me slyly. And wiggled her arse.

—Anything you want before I put it all away.

Susan

I'm not quite sure how it happened but I was naked. Lying flat. The damask cold against my back. My legs were bent at the knees over the edge of the table. Phillip had pulled up a chair and sat down. For whatever reason, he wasn't satisfied. He pushed the chair back again and crossed the shop to where an upholstered footstool was sitting with some other smaller pieces of furniture. Back at the table, he positioned the stool carefully beneath my dangling feet.

When he sat down this time, his head was at table level. Pussy level. He slid his hands down my legs and gently lifted my ankles over his shoulders. He held on to my thighs and pulled me forward. My body glided effortlessly—the damask runner providing an ornate conveyer belt that floated over the polished wood with ease.

His tongue went into me, accurately finding the spot without hesitation. It made me gasp. I tried to raise my head to look down at him but all I could see was the top of *his* head. Gently bobbing. The corresponding movement of his tongue creating holy havoc in me. I let my head fall back on the table, saw the chandelier briefly before closing my eyes, and then I let his good deed wash all over me. I gripped the edge of the table. Felt the drawer handle. And smiled.

There was a spoon in the drawer. The one I had been saving to show him—the one that gave a whole new meaning to "spooning" with your lover.

James

Susan had never been particularly enthusiastic about my family. So I wasn't surprised she turned up her nose at the thought of celebrating my octogenarian Auntie Lucy's birthday with me in London. But when I suggested she simply stop in on the way to the Paris Antiques Fair, just to make an appearance, she troubled me by saying she wasn't sure if she was going to the fair.

Maybe she's worn herself out. She's been working late at the shop a lot recently.

Susan

I was a bit ambivalent about going to the Spring Antiques Fair in Paris this year. I normally always enjoyed it. I loved the people. Meeting up with European dealers. There were always good collections. Pieces that you didn't find anywhere else. And of course, the shopping and my special moisturizer to buy.

But this year was different. And it was all because of Phillip.

I was getting laid on a regular basis now and I seriously didn't want it to stop.

Not even for a few days while I was in Paris.

The best sex in your life comes later in life! I'll drink to that.

I had fantasized about Phillip coming to France with me but dismissed it as schoolgirl foolishness. But now, after more than two months of horizontal hijinks with him, it seemed more plausible.

Plus, there was the not insignificant fact that Phillip worshipped my body.

When I sat astride him, he would look up and place his hands either side of my rib cage. He would let them drift down and in, following my waistline and then out again as he traced the curves of my hips.

–I love this, he would say. –You have a young girl's figure, the clichéd hourglass.

And then he would reach up and cup my breasts in his hands.

–You're so fucking beautiful, Susan.

All the while, I was sliding slowly up and down on him. Raising my shoulders on the way up. Twisting them on the way down. He never took his eyes off me.

–How long will you be gone? Phillip had asked during a phone conversation.

–If I go, four or five days.

–Will James go?

–Yes and no. We'd probably fly to London together. He's spending time with his family there. A great aunt's birthday. But I'd connect straight on to Paris and fly back directly from there. James will fly home from London.

–So you're not spending time with his family?

–I prefer not to, Phillip. Take that as you want, I said.

I was family-ed out with James's clan. He was welcome to them all. Phillip had gone silent. And then he spoke with a certain naughtiness in his voice.

–Why don't I fly directly to Paris and meet you?

I got excited. In every way.

–You'd do that?

–I'd do anything to be with you, Susan.

And so that made up my mind and it was all arranged.

James and I would fly to London on the Monday. I would continue by myself to Paris to attend the opening days of the Fair on Tuesday and Wednesday—the days reserved for dealers only. Phillip would arrive Wednesday evening from New York. We'd meet at the *Hotel du Danube*, my hotel, strictly for a business meeting. I would keep my room there but we'd walk over to another hotel where I wasn't known and where we could discreetly check in together under his name. I would take him to the public viewings at the Fair on Thursday. It would actually be fun for him to see how silver was bought and sold. He might actually learn something! He had surprised me by showing a genuine interest in his collection. It was no longer just a *means to get his end away* as he put it. We would have a weekend together and fly back Sunday afternoon.

Then it all fell apart.

I was crossing the lobby of the hotel a little after 10:30 on Wednesday morning and suddenly James appeared.

–What are you doing here?

–Nice greeting.

I kissed him lightly on the cheek.

—Sorry, James. But I was hardly expecting to see you.

—I went to my auntie's birthday last night. It was all very nice. Upstairs at L'Escargot in Soho. And then some of us went to Kettner's afterwards. I was surprised to find it was still pretty much the same, other than the fact it's a vodka bar now.

—Not champagne any longer?

—Well, yes. But vodka as well. It's what all the younger people are drinking these days. With clever names like *Kremlin* and *Oddka*. Anyway. I got thinking about you. How you told me that Kettner's was where all the girls took you before we got married and I suddenly got rather nostalgic.

—For Kettner's? I said a little impatiently.

James sighed.

—For you, Susan. And so I took the 6:18 morning Chunnel over. It goes out of St. Pancras now, just a short cab ride from Covent Garden. We pulled into Paris Nord bang on time at 9:47 and here I am. Surprise! Surprise!

Surprise fucking surprise! Holy crap. I kissed him again.

—And you're staying?

—For a few days. Then I'll go back to London and fly to New York from there as planned.

He paused and thought for a second.

—Or I suppose I could fly directly back from here. Let's not decide now.

I had to call Phillip. Really fucking quickly. There was still time to stop him.

I said a hurried goodbye to James blaming the need to work. I rushed over to the Fair. There was an office there for dealers to use. Like the business centers in big hotels. Phone. Internet. Scanning. Faxing.

It was now coming up to 5:00 in the morning in New York. Phillip's flight was leaving at 8:00.

He would still be at home. Probably just got up and doing last-minute packing.

Please. Let it be.

Phillip

The phone rang at the same time the alarm went off. Double bells in my head.

That's what I drank in England. A double Bells whisky. It's funny how drinking thoughts never go away for an alcoholic. I shut off the alarm and picked up the phone.

–Hello?

–Thank fuck I've got you. It's Susan.

I laughed.

–I know. The only other person who would call me at this hour would be my darling sister. I was just getting up.

–Don't.

Susan said it rather sharply.

–What's wrong, Susan?

–You can't come to Paris.

–Why ever not?

–James has suddenly shown up.

–Oh, shit!

–Oh, shit is right. But at least I caught you. Look, don't call me. I'll call you when I can. Tonight, maybe. I must go. Goodbye, Phillip.

–Goodbye, Susan.

I put the phone down. Crap. Crappitty crap. I picked it up again, called Air France, cancelled my flight, and said *au revoir* to best laid plans. Best *laid* being the operative. When I climbed back into bed, J.C. climbed on it as well and I didn't have the heart to throw him off. I lay on my back, thinking.

This was going to be the moment.

Paris.

When I asked Susan to leave James and be with me. She would say: *Yes!* Completely swept up by the magic of the city and the moment.

She told me not to call. I'd write to her instead, a heart-felt fax. I would mark it Private and Confidential—*Privé et Confidentiel.*

Susan

James and I came down to the little lobby of the *Danube* early Thursday morning. There were bigger, fancier places, but this little left bank hotel was our place. We had a dirty weekend here before we were married. Before we were even engaged! *Quelle horreur!* It had always been special to us and that made me feel even more awful about the night before.

Phone sex with Phillip again.

I said I would call him and before I knew it, he had seduced me via his cell. This time, on the balcony outside our room, overlooking the streets of *Saint-Germain-Des-Prés*.

Des-Prés loosely translates to *in the meadows*.

So we were fucking in the meadows! Lovely. Once more, the idea that James was nearby—the danger of it—excited me. Oh dear, oh dear, Susan. What were you thinking?

James wanted to take a morning stroll and pick up an *International Herald Tribune*. He actually spoke French rather well. Enough to get by as he put it, in a bar or restaurant. But reading the language was a chore for him. And so *Le Monde* had no appeal. I would meet him at the little café next door.

As we crossed the lobby, I noticed the night porter, Jerome, was still on duty. He saw us and called out from behind the front desk. There was something about him I didn't like.

—*Monsieur, un fax pour vous.*

We stopped in the center of the lobby by the mahogany table that was decorated with huge bunches of fresh flowers from *Les Halles*. I looked at James. He looked at Jerome.

—*Pour moi? Étes-vous sûrs, Jerome?*

—Were you expecting a fax, James? I asked.

—No, I can't think who it would be from. Only you know I changed my plans. I left so early yesterday I didn't even tell my family. Let me take a look.

James turned to the front desk. I leaned down to smell a rose. Phillip had given me roses before I left along with a

125

poem he had written for me—*The Rose Knows.*

–The rose knows, and my nose knows, the sweet scent of you, he had read in a seductive tone.

Oh, my god! Phillip!

I rushed over to the desk just as Jerome was handing James the fax. Thank goodness Jerome had folded it and put it in one of the hotel's buff envelopes, monogrammed proudly in gold with the hotel logo.

–It's for me. It's for me, James. From Sarah.

James looked wide-eyed at me. It must have seemed that I had gone quite mad. An outburst in the middle of the lobby. I snatched the envelope that was midway into James' outstretched hand.

–Goodness, Susan. It must be important.

–Yes. Sorry, yes. Didn't mean to grab it like that.

James looked down at the envelope. Jerome had marked it simply: *Birley. Privé et Confidentiel.* No first initial. James looked at me quizzically.

–I'll see you next door in a while, he said softly.

Jerome gave me a half-smile. Mischievous. Or devious, depending on your point of view I guess.

That *bâtard.*

He had read the fax. I didn't know what was in it. But he did. And was he really going to give it to James? Give me away? What has happened to this hotel? Give me the reliable porters of old. The ones whose middle name was *Discretion.*

My heart was beating faster than a fucking hummingbird's wings. I headed out the hotel and turned right to the café. I paused before going in to compose myself.

Rue Jacob was coming alive.

The pavement in front of the antique store across the street was being hosed down. Lifeless *Gauloises* butts were being forced by the powerful jet of water into the gutter where they would wait for the street cleaning truck already moving slowly down the street towards them.

The students from the *Universite de Paris* zoomed around

on their mopeds. Those on foot congregated in front of the university doors as they did every school day, waiting for their classes to start. They were laughing and smoking, and this being Paris, kissing openly. Boy to girl. Girl to girl. Boy to boy.

Some headed towards the café where they would linger over just one *café au lait* for what seemed like hours. I loved this French custom. Buy a coffee and you've rented the table for as long as you wanted it. No one to hurry you out because other people were waiting. The others can just jolly well hold their horses or drink at the bar. And it's cheaper at the bar anyway. Cheaper by half. I loved this too. No chair? Then no charge for sitting. I've tried to imagine how this would go down in America. New York bar and restaurant owners would just laugh at the thought.

The café's other early morning customers were the men in dark blue coveralls that kept the city working along with a smattering of local businessmen.

Rue Jacob housed mainly antiques shops, art galleries, and restoration workshops. Another reason I liked to stay at *Hôtel du Danube*.

I entered the café and nodded good morning to a silversmith I knew standing at the bar. He was enjoying his morning *goutte*. His *réveillez l'appel*. The wake-up call.

I could never quite fathom the idea of a beer or an *eau de vie* first thing in the morning, but these men seemed perfectly happy with theirs. I'm sure Phillip knew all about it. Vodka and cornflakes, he had once said. *Rise and shine!*

I found a table in the corner by the window and sat down with a *café au lait*.

It was unseasonably warm and the windows—doors actually—were opened out and folded back. The street poured in and the smell of the café poured out. I sat precisely where the two currents met.

I pushed my cup off to one side and laid the envelope containing the fax on the table. I had pretty much destroyed the envelope in my panicked grasp. I had an open view of the street here all the way down to the corner and I took a quick look for James. Nowhere yet.

I picked up a knife from the table and slipped the point under one corner of the envelope. In one swift movement, the knife slid along the top of the envelope like, well, like a knife through butter.

I pried open the slit edges the knife had left in its wake and peered inside. A sheet of the hotel paper. White though. Not the buff color of the envelope. Plain old white fax paper. I removed it from the envelope, put the envelope out of sight in my bag and smoothed out the fax on the café table. If James were to show up while I was reading, the fax would easily follow the envelope into my bag.

At the top of the page was an illustration. Two inches deep and about an inch wide. The fax machine's limited printing ability had not done justice to the picture.

It was a black and white version of a Marc Chagall painting. I knew the painting well. It was called *The Wedding* and he had painted it in 1910 for his bride to be. I couldn't remember if the wedding ever happened; I don't think it did. Under the picture was a single column of type. Elegant italics.

A poem. I had told Phillip I liked *The Rose Knows* and now he had composed another rhyme. Very sweet. But what the fuck was he thinking?

Why would he send it to the hotel when he knew James was with me? I was furious and touched at the same time. Which pretty much summed up the whole relationship, didn't it?

Furious at myself for cheating on James. But touched and mesmerized by Phillip's romantic antics.

Just as I started to read, my attention was drawn away to the door. I thought it was James at first, but it was a man of similar height backing into the café. He was pulling a hand trolley, which bumped over the well-worn wooden step leading to the small entry space. The trolley was stacked with bags of coffee beans. *The coffee man in the café.* The thought tickled me. Rather than unload his delivery, he walked along the bar and nodded to the men who were propping it up. A *bonjour* here, a *c'est va?* there.

The café owner pushed a small white porcelain cup towards him. No saucer. Steaming *espresso*. Turning to the bottles stacked behind the bar, the owner selected one, took two small shot-like glasses from under the bar, and filled each of them to the brim. He re-corked the bottle and put it back in place before saluting his deliveryman. The glasses were emptied in one and placed with a bang on the old pewter bar. No words were exchanged. Only the quick signing of a delivery slip.

Whoops! This unique slice of Parisian life had distracted me. Right, girl. Get back to the fax before James walks in.

Together?

Oh, no. I knew from the title what was coming. My stomach lurched.

Please. Don't do this, Phillip.

We're having an affair.

That's *all*.

Please don't say what I think you're going to say.

I reached for the little bowl of sugar cubes on the table and plopped one in my coffee. Then I decided I needed a second. Or maybe even a *goutte*. I read on.

Do you
Or don't you?
Will you
Or won't you?
Can we
Or can't we?
Shall we
Or shan't we?
Are we
Or aren't we?

Together?
That of course,
Remains
To be seen.

Christ, Phillip. I could hear him saying the words, filling in the missing parts of the poem.

Do you (love me)
Or don't you?
Will you (leave James)
Or won't you?
Can we (get on with this)
Or can't we?
Shall we (be married)
Or shan't we?
(Well, Susan) Are we
Or aren't we?
Together?

And then a clever reference to the name of my own fucking shop. I hated it. I loved it. I screwed it up in the palm of my hand and threw it into my bag. I was angry. James came through the door.

–What the hell is wrong with you this morning, Susan? First you rip faxes from my hand and now you're sitting here looking like you're ready to commit murder.

–I'm sorry, James. I don't know what's wrong. Time of life all over again, I guess.

James sat down and ordered his coffee.

Sarah

I got the strangest phone call from James.

He said he was in Paris and was letting me know that Susan had got my fax.

–My fax? I said, with an obvious question mark.

Susan

Despite his apparent determination to slam into every other vehicle on the road, the cab driver got us to *Charles de Gaulle* airport in one piece.

Leaving the hotel was a bit traumatic all round. There was no point in staying on after the last day of the fair now. I changed my flight to get back on Friday. I was furious at Phillip for sending me the fax but I did actually love it at the same time. It gave me little bit of power. And he liked me to be in control. I would scold him. Fuck him. And then tell him to forget any romantic notions; that this relationship, if you could call it that, was only about sex. It was bonking or be gone.

At the last minute James decided he was going to come back to America with me and not return to his family in London after all. This meant more phone calls to the airlines, canceling bookings, and then re-booking. It also meant I had to delay checking out of the hotel. The limo I booked for myself turned up but couldn't wait while James packed—*un autre emploi*—and left. Then there was a bit of a fuss getting a cab to come. We hit the usual morning rush hour traffic in the center of Paris, and so all in all, it was amazing we arrived at the airport at all.

A rather attractive young lady at check-in told us very politely that the airport was in the middle of a wildcat strike by baggage handlers and that our flight was delayed by several hours. But not to worry—it would certainly leave before the end of the day.

We finally boarded five hours later and I collapsed into my seat. There had been no announcements other than to tell us to stay close to the gate at all times as we would be boarding within minutes of the dispute being settled.

I now desperately wanted a vodka. They were only serving champagne and or champagne and orange juice in business class. I could see through to first class and they were getting what I wanted: cocktails and lots of them. I would make do with champagne. James declined and I took his as well. I opted for straight champagne. No need to waste valuable room in the glass by mixing in orange juice.

We were now flying west with the night. My thoughts turned to New York and Phillip.

I still couldn't quite believe Phillip had sent me a marriage proposal. A proposal of some sort, anyway.

Good Lord! What was he thinking? What *is* he thinking? Once again, I knew exactly what I was thinking: I'm going to have to slow things down as soon as I get back. Be straightforward with him.

–*This is an affair, Phillip. That's all. I'm not leaving James. I don't want to get divorced. I don't want to marry you. Or even live with you!*

I finally got my vodka after takeoff. With that on top of the hastily quaffed champagne, the situation with Phillip was now sounding very easy to handle. I looked across at James. He was sleeping peacefully. Blissfully unaware, as they say. Oh, James. Dearest, sweetest, James.

I had had sex more times with Phillip over the last few months than I had in years with James. And quite frankly, I loved it.

But not enough to upset my lifestyle.

James and I were comfortable together in every sense.

Phillip would understand. He loved the sex as well. I'd deal with the romantic notions that seemed to be swirling around in his poet's head and we'd get back to some good, earthy shagging as they say these days.

I woke with a start as the plane bumped down in New York. We taxied for an eternity and then seemed to wait forever a good distance from the terminal. Nothing but terminal waiting today, I suppose.

The captain came on finally.

–Ladies and Gentlemen, I just wanted to welcome you to a rainy JFK. Because of our late arrival, we have to wait for a gate. I have been told it could be up to thirty minutes.

A collective groan went up from the passengers as the

captain continued, telling us that he would keep us fully informed of the situation.

A few minutes later he was back. It wasn't what we wanted to hear.

−Well, I'm afraid I misspoke just then. I shouldn't have said *up to* thirty minutes but *at least* thirty minutes. It may even be more like an hour.

I was too tired to groan with the others this time. They did a good enough job without my help. James sat through it all very calmly. The captain pressed on.

−The good news is that the tower has given me permission to waive federal regulations and allow you to use your cell phones in case you need to. As a reminder, please be courteous to those sitting around you.

Up yours, everyone obviously thought as they dived for their mobiles.

I reached down and took mine from my carry-on bag. I pressed the power button and the screen came alive. The message icon was blinking furiously. I tapped *Retrieve,* put the phone to my ear, and looked at James. He was staring out the window at the rain. Water was beginning to form beads on the double layer of glass and he seemed to watching the journey of one particular bead as it made its way from the top of the window to the bottom. Phillip's voice suddenly rang in my ear. It was loud. Loud enough to make James look up. I quickly switched the phone away from my right side, where James was sitting, to my left ear. James looked puzzled. As if he had caught the words.

−Susan, I love you.

I squeezed the phone tighter to my ear in an effort to muffle the sound.

James looked away again. I pushed delete, and listened to the next message.

−It's Phillip again. I'm at the airport. I thought I'd surprise you by greeting you off the plane but your plane's been delayed several hours and I'm going to have to get back home soon. Depending on what time they finally estimate your arrival, I may or not be there. Good intentions and all that. Can't wait to kiss you when I see you.

Delete. Next message. Phillip again. William fucking Shakespeare this time though.

Our eyes, then our hearts,
Our bodies we tethered.
Together at last,
And at last, we're together.

I hung up. I couldn't bear to listen to any more. And I didn't want James to overhear anything. What is going on with Phillip? I wondered whether he'd been drinking again, maybe that was why he was acting irrationally. Not because he'd fallen in love with me but because he was drinking.

I thought I felt sorry for him when he told me the story of his alcoholism. But now? Well, I couldn't make a commitment to an alcoholic, could I? Period.

There was the usual out of the starting-gate race when we finally got to the terminal. A ding-dong followed by frantic flinging back of overhead bins, the retrieving of luggage, and the aisle filled with people stepping on each other's toes. And then nothing. Because as usual, it seemed that someone had forgotten to mention to the ground crew that there was a plane waiting to unload, that there were two hundred passengers about to mutiny, and maybe they should open the fucking doors.

All this time I had been furiously painting different scenarios. What if Phillip had waited? I couldn't go through without James to warn Phillip that my husband was with me. Phillip had never met James and had no idea what he looked like. On top of that, James always walked with me in such a detached manner, you'd sometimes never know we were together. Phillip probably wouldn't put the two of us together either.

Fuck! Phillip wouldn't have a sign, would he?
I LOVE YOU SUSAN! MARRY ME!

I would kill him. Steady on, girl. You're getting a little carried away here, aren't you? Don't project. There won't be a sign. There won't be any sign of Phillip either.

We went through immigration, got our bags, and cleared customs. The silver I had bought was being shipped so there was nothing to declare.

I pushed my trolley through the swing doors and took a deep breath. James was two paces behind me.

Phillip was stupid. Stupid. Stupid. Stupid.

He's not here. Good. Good.

—James. I'm in the long-term car park. Do you want to wait here with the luggage? I'll drive round.

—No, that's okay. I want some air. I'll push.

James and I came out into the street and it was raining heavily now. We hurried against the traffic light and crossed the road to the parking lot. I spotted the Range Rover and walked towards it quickly, getting as far away from James as I could in the short distance.

I pushed the button on the key fob and the doors unlocked with a simultaneous *shungggg*.

And then I saw it.

Held in place against the windshield by the wipers was a big white card: WELCOME HOME, SUSAN. The rain had made its inky letters run. Like Halloween lettering. Like the nightmare that this journey home had become.

Oh, Jesus. He had really been here with a fucking welcome sign. Shit.

James, mercifully, had stopped by the tailgate ready to load the luggage. He had his head in the back and didn't see me hastily remove the sign, drop it to the ground, and push it under the car with my foot.

We would drive off and leave it there to be driven over by the next car that parked in the space. James would be none the wiser.

Phillip, you fucking idiot. It's over.

Phillip

Bloody Nora! Susan was right royally pissed off. I obviously misread the whole thing.

I thought she had gone out of her way to let me know what flight she was on because she wanted me to meet her. That she was talking in code on the phone from Paris because James was nearby. I honestly thought she wanted me to be there with a big bunch of flowers and a passionate embrace—*not* that she wanted me to stay away. When the plane was delayed, I simply drove around the long-term parking lot until I found her car and left her the *Welcome Home!* sign. And how was I supposed to know that James was with her? When we spoke, she said he was going to go back to London for a few more days. She sounded very pissed off at him as well. Which wasn't necessarily a bad thing. That could work in my favor. We didn't see each other over the weekend—she said she needed to let things settle down with James a bit. In case he had overheard anything. Suspected anything. She would take care of business on the home front again and then we'd meet for lunch at our usual spot—*Bistro Bijoux*—and talk. And that's what we did. Susan had calmed down now and was in a good mood.

–Will you tell James, Susan?

–I have to do this my way, Phillip.

That was a yes. No doubt about it. I wouldn't say anything more. I wouldn't push it. She would do it her way and then we'd be together. I got the check, paid, and scribbled on the back of the receipt.

–Writing the lunch off against your taxes?

–Just a reminder of who I'm with and what I'm spending. Part of my sobriety is to be disciplined.

Susan literally purred.

–Talking of which, Phillip. I liked that spanking you gave me before I went to Paris. What are you doing this afternoon?

—Spanking someone?

—Well, I have a thought. I have a mirror in the back of the car that I have to deliver. Come with me. We'll deliver it and then see what happens.

I was happy. We'd got over the hump of the past few days and now we were about to embark on a hump of a different kind.

A few minutes later we were in the Range Rover heading over to the very smart town of Lincolnville.

Susan rarely talked about her customers to me. It would have been a bit of a breach in a way. Some people don't want it known how much they spend on antiques. They hide their money in them. Away from the prying eyes of the IRS. If they buy wisely from someone discreet like Susan, they can easily sell back in times of need. And even though flipping was publicly frowned upon—buying from a dealer and then selling back to the same dealer—it happened all the time.

The dealer gets a commission by selling a piece to Buyer One. Then Buyer One makes a profit by selling it back to the same dealer at a higher price. The dealer has already teased another client, Buyer Two, that something special is coming on the market. As long as Buyer Two is willing to pay a slightly inflated price, everybody is happy. Smart dealers have customers lined up in two tiers for this very purpose. The first tier always buys about market price. The second tier has more money than sense and will pay anything. And this little piggy (the dealer) goes wee, wee, wee, all the way home having pocketed two commissions from selling the same piece.

We pulled up to a pair of huge iron gates. Susan lowered the window and leaned into a speaker box. She announced herself. The gates opened and we went through.

—What if your customer sees me? Won't he be pissed off that you brought me up to his house with an expensive piece for all to see?

Susan gave me a withering look.

—Phillip, I wouldn't do that. Anyway, he's not here. He's in the Turks and Caicos. He has a house there and spends February and March on the islands before coming back to Chester for a few months in the spring. Then he flies to Tuscany for the balance of the summer. Fall, Christmas, and the New Year are spent in New England, and then it's off to the tropics again.

—Life's a bastard, eh?

Susan laughed.

—You could say that. He grew up in an orphanage. Never knew who his parents were. Left school at fifteen and shoved it to the world by becoming a billionaire by the time he was thirty. Tech biz, naturally. Now he owns a football team, a news service, private clubs, restaurants, and real estate down in the Turks, which has fast become a winter playground for the rich and famous. Here's his manservant.

I looked up and saw a beautiful girl. Long red hair. Ample amounts of everything except clothing.

—Manservant?

—That's what my client calls her. She's a servant to her man, I guess. He has a whole stable of them back there. Red smiled and waved at Susan.

Susan stopped and got out and hugged her—a little longer than what some people might have considered polite.

Red gestured to two gardeners working nearby and they came over as Susan opened up the Range Rover's tailgate. She pulled back a blanket to reveal the crated mirror.

With the seats folded flat, there was a lot of room in the back. The size of a bed, Susan had once said.

The gardeners carefully removed the crate and carried it into the house. Actually, mansion.

Susan kissed Red again and got back in the car. I guess there was no need to introduce me. I didn't say anything about that but I had a question.

—Don't you have to go in and show them how to take it out of the crate? If it's that valuable?

—It's not coming out of the crate. It will either be sent to the Turks by a shipper I recommended who has a judicious understanding of my client's need for privacy, or it will go into a vault where it will remain untouched and unopened. My client doesn't even know what it looks like. I just told him he should have it and he said yes. Drop it off at the house, he said. He was calling from the beach at the time.

This explained a lot about Susan.

The world she moved in was clearly a *you want it, you got it* kind of place. She started the Range Rover.

—Okay, Spanky. Let's do it.

Susan seemed happy. She said very little as she drove through the winding country lanes, past all the big horse farms and mansions. She pointed out homes she had sold various antiques to.

—They have a pair of Queen Anne side chairs of mine. These people have a Georgian chandelier of mine. This man has an Irish card table of mine—walnut, Victorian.

Even though Susan had sold them, she obviously still considered these *her* pieces. As if they were on loan.

We drove down a hedge-lined driveway and stopped in the middle of nowhere. She got out of the car.

—Come on. Hurry.

She opened the tailgate again but this time climbed in. I followed her and she pulled the tailgate down from the inside.

—What if someone comes along? What if someone sees us?

—We'll hide under the blanket that was covering the mirror. Stop being such a *Nancy Boy* and get your beautiful dick out.

Phillip

I got up late the next morning and went down the driveway with J.C. to get the newspaper.

While he was going about his morning routine against the bushes, I looked in the mailbox.

There was a note from Susan. Hand-delivered. Hand-written. A hurried message on a sheet of her letterhead.

She wants meet again. Tomorrow. *Bistro Bijoux*. She must have spoken to James.

Susan

I fucked in the back of the Range Rover.
Phillip made love.
This can't go on.
I left a note in his mailbox very early this morning.

Hope for Tomorrow.

Skyward I glance.
You, on my mind.
I find a grey sky
Of the stormiest kind.
Turbulent grey.
The grey of sorrow.
Though the sun is hidden
There's hope for tomorrow.

Susan will leave James. Her way.
So why am I so anxious?

Phillip

I am the only customer in an English country pub. Wide-plank floors and low-beamed ceilings. The lingering smell of yesterday's beer and cigarettes mixes with the fragrant lavender polish the cleaning lady is rubbing into well-worn wooden tables. It is just past opening time, 11:00 in the morning. My favorite hour. Through the leaded window, I can see acres and acres of rolling fields dotted with an occasional oak. The barman has just set down a foaming pint on the scarred and gouged mahogany bar in front of me. I slide a five-pound note across to him and he turns to the till. As I bring the glass to my mouth, I close my eyes in anticipation. But before I can savor that first lick of foaming white froth, the first mouthful of beer that sweeps away all the cobwebs from the night before, the bloody till emits a loud and unrelenting beep.

I woke with a start.

I forgot to turn the alarm off. Beep. Beep. Beep. The unrelenting beep of my dream. I had been having drinking dreams for a few days now. They seem so real. I am drinking and I know I shouldn't be drinking, but I can't help it.

Sometimes I'm in a pub in England. Sometimes by myself at home. Always a feeling of guilt.

Wanting a drink. Not wanting it. Taking it and then feeling anguish. Throwing away my sobriety.

I'm not going to let that happen.

One day at a time. This too shall pass. Easy does it. All the AA clichés actually work. They keep people sober.

Quite often, drinking dreams are simply a reflection of some sort of stress an alcoholic is going through. I've been through a stressful time with Susan. I'll go to a lunchtime AA meeting and surround myself with sober people. It'll be good for me. Keep things calm. There will be time to go to the Methodist Church in Kimpton where the meeting is held and then meet Susan at 1:30 in Old Woodford. A late lunch. In England, a late lunch was a euphemism for drinking all afternoon, not just the lateness of the hour.

It will be a momentous lunch though. We will celebrate the beginning of our new life together. I have asked Susan to leave James. She said she would do it. Her way. My darling Susan who had told me in Newport that she never wanted it to end.

—*I never want this to end, Phillip.*

Her exact words.

I had been working all morning and just as I was leaving for AA, Jennifer called. We were on the phone for more than forty-five minutes. She surprised me by telling me she had met someone and they had moved into a house in West Hollywood already. She was happy. I didn't tell her about Susan leaving James. She didn't know any details anyway. All she knew was that I was shagging a married woman, a Mrs. Not much more than that. No need to go into the nitty-gritty. By the time we had hung up, I had missed most of the AA meeting. I was feeling okay though. If I felt unsafe, I'd call my sponsor. His was the first number on my cell phone's speed dial. Calling sponsor. Calling sponsor. I decided to drive straight to the restaurant.

Bistro Bijoux was very close to *Remains To Be Seen* which meant Susan could pop out for lunch without leaving the shop for too long. Convenient yes, and dangerously close at the same. But we considered it hiding in plain sight.

Susan always brought a couple of silver spoons or a piece of china with her that she displayed prominently on the table. If we should bump into anyone we knew, we were having a business lunch. Simple as that.

We learned to talk about each other's bodies in a matter of fact way with a perfectly straight face. I, for instance, might pick up one the pieces she had brought with her, examine the maker's mark carefully and without looking up, simply say:

—Patterson. 1813. Dundee. By the way, did I mention that you have abso-bloody-lutely fantastic tits?

I liked *Bistro Bijoux*. The name remained from the restaurant's early days when the owner served simple French cooking in a modest setting. Some years back, its humble roots were dropped and *Bistro Bijoux* emerged—a gorgeous jewel of a restaurant in every respect. *Handsome decor, subtle lighting, intimate dining spaces and fabulous flowers. All this makes a fitting backdrop for the civilized hum of conversation and for dining on some brilliantly executed dishes.* It got the kind of rave reviews from the *New York Times* restaurateurs die for.

Today the restaurant was very busy and the *civilized hum of conversation* had been lost on a group of four ladies. They arrived one at a time and as they greeted each other, their noise level escalated to a point where they were practically shouting. Like drunks in a bar at the end of an evening— thinking they were simply talking to each other when in fact, they were yelling at the tops of their voices.

I looked away just as Susan approached the table where I was waiting. She looked beautiful. A black skirt, just to her knees. An elegantly cut *MaxMara* tweed jacket over a black blouse. A simple gold chain around her neck. I loved her.

—Are you wearing knickers?

—Stop it, Phillip.

There was an edge to her voice I didn't recognize. Firm, angry, upset. All at the same time.

I stood up and pulled the chair opposite me away from the table. She sat down. Even in that simple action, and I had seen it hundreds of times, there was a difference. A brusqueness if that's possible. She banged a silver snuffbox down on the table. The force flipped its lid open. I reached across, picked up the piece, closed the lid again, and without looking into her eyes, spoke quietly.

—Did you tell him?

—No.

—Did you try to tell him?

—No, Phillip. There was no need.

I read all kinds of things into this statement. This explained her anger. Her upset.

James must already know about us.

—He already knows? He wants a divorce? He asked first? Before you had a chance to ask him?

She looked at me as if I had two heads.

—Phillip!

—What?

—Of course he didn't ask for a bloody divorce. And neither did I. Phillip, I'm not leaving him.

—Why not? You said you would.

I immediately knew I sounded pathetic. Like a child who hasn't got his way. Sherry, who had served us before, was all smiles as she came over to the table, as if pleased to see us again.

—Are you ready to hear the specials?

—No, go away.

Susan glared and then snapped at me.

—Phillip. Don't be rude!

Susan turned to Sherry who, naturally, was taken aback by my outburst.

—Give us a few minutes would you please, Sherry?

Sherry's scan of me suggested that she was going to return from the kitchen in the allotted *few minutes* with the chef's sharpest knife and relieve me of my now faltering manhood in one swift slice. She turned away, shaking her head.

Susan looked at me with eyes I didn't recognize. I fingered the snuffbox. It was a lovely piece. I squeezed the sides, which activated a hidden spring and opened the lid. It was clever. They knew what they were doing two hundred years ago. I assumed it was Georgian.

I closed it, squeezed it again, and the lid sprang open once more. I was like that petulant kid again, not looking at his parents but repeating an action he knew would tick them off. Sure enough.

—Don't play with that, Phillip. You'll break it.

—I'm not a child, Susan.

—You're acting like one.

–Susan, I love you. I want to be with you. I thought we agreed. When we were in Newport you said you never wanted it to end. It doesn't have to and it won't if you leave James. We could be together. Happily ever after and all that. I thought it was all very adult.

–I know exactly what I said in Newport, Phillip. I meant I didn't want the weekend to end.

–Just the weekend? Come on, Susan. Give me a break. Tell me the truth. You've simply changed your mind, right? Admit it.

–No. Yes. Well, no. Phillip, I was never going to leave James. Regardless of what I might have said in–

–Oh, the old *spoken in a moment of passion* thing. Hot and heavy. I meant it at the time and all that. And what about the *I'm going to do it my way* promise? Don't tell me now that doing it your way was the sexual equivalent of having your cake and eating it. Fuck Phillip's brains out but enjoy your safe old life with James.

Susan put her face in her hands and shook her head making her beautifully cut hair swing from side to side. She looked up. The intensity with which her fingers had cupped her lovely face had left red marks around her eyes and on her cheeks.

–Don't make this more difficult than it already is.

–Susan, don't you love me?

Sherry was back. She was only holding her notepad, no glinting chef's knife. Susan wasn't taking any chances of another scene being made over the simple act of ordering. She didn't let me speak but smiled her best smile at Sherry.

–We'll both have the chicken *paillard* salad, Sherry. No fries.

–I want fries.

The child again.

–Give him fries.

Susan all but said it will keep him quiet.

Sherry was enjoying this. –Two chicken *paillard* salads. And French fries for the little guy.

Sherry turned away giggling. I would be the laughing stock of the kitchen staff within a few minutes. I repeated the question.

–Susan, don't you love me?

Susan simply shook her head again.

–This is my fault, Phillip–

–This isn't about fault, Susan, I cut in.

–Let me finish.

She said it firmly. I knew I should shut up. She continued.

–Phillip. I pursued you. The silver collection was my way of getting you to come–

–I know all that…sorry…I interrupted again.

–To come back to the shop, she continued. –I wanted you. I wanted your body. You came to love mine. You did things to me, touched me, spoke to me in ways I hadn't experienced for years. In ways I had never, ever, ever enjoyed before. You made it all right for me to say things like: I'm wet. You offered me excitement, Phillip. I was swept away by your attention. Your phone calls. Your lovemaking. Even your poetry! Oh god, Phillip.

–But was that really all it was? Sex?

–No, Phillip. You're not listening to me. You made me come alive. At a time in my life when I was desperately unhappy. But I have come to realize that I could never leave James. Never. When I was on the plane to the U.K. after I first met you, I felt that I had been married to James all my life. And that seemed a bad thing. Now I realize I *have* been married to James all my life. And it's a good thing.

–You sound like some domestic diva.

Susan let out a deep sigh.

–Phillip, where has this sarcasm come from?

–Where has the sarcasm come from? Where the fuck do you think it's come from?

–Please don't swear.

–Why the fuck not? Where the fuck do you think the sarcasm has come from, Susan? You pursued me, as you said. You told me you loved the idea of me. Oh sorry. That was just in a moment of heated passion, wasn't it? It was only the *idea* of me, obviously. You said your marriage had left you tired and disappointed. You said just a few moments ago that I put excitement in your life. And now you're telling me that–

Susan stopped me dead. Took control of the conversation again. The control I used to like. But this time she did it by speaking with a gentle sincerity.

–That I won't leave James? That's right, Phillip. That's what I'm telling you. And do you know what? If there was a way of continuing, of just satisfying each other's basic needs with no strings attached, I would do it in a heartbeat, Phillip. I love your cock. See, you've even made it okay for me to say things like that. But you want more, Phillip. And I can't give you what you want. I don't want to hurt you anymore. I don't want to hurt James. He needs me. And so it's a case of all or nothing.

–The Small Faces. 1966.

Susan ignored the musicology. On another occasion, she might have marveled at me being able to pull the band name and dates of a hit song like *All or Nothing* out of thin air. Not now. I didn't know why I had said it either. It was totally inappropriate. I felt stupid. I just sighed. I tried to get the conversation back on track but the schoolboy appeared again.

–Well, it's fine for you. You can go home to your husband. To James. And I'll just go back to an empty house and my dog. This is going to be a lot easier for you than me, Susan. I don't have someone else in my life.

–Oh, Phillip. Please, darling.

–Two chicken *paillards*. Would you like ketchup for the fries, sweetie?

–Fuck off.

Susan said nothing this time. Sherry had got my goat and she knew it. Worse still, she loved it. She wasn't in the least bit offended by me telling her to go forth and multiply. She simply smiled sweetly.

We ate. In total silence. The sound of the knives and forks our only accompaniment. Lots of gazing anywhere but at each other. Deliberate eating. Deliberately avoiding eye contact. And then we were finished. Susan had actually eaten hers. This awful conversation must have made her hungry. I simply pushed most of mine around the plate. Sherry came, said nothing, and just took the plates away. She had won the game and there was no need to twist the knife anymore. She left desert menus on the table. Darker in shade, but the same pink color used for the tablecloths. Susan got up.

—I have to get back. Call me later. We have to talk more.

I was very quiet now. Very by myself. I was on the verge of crying. I closed my eyes and opened them slowly. I spoke almost without sound. I was dying inside. A thousand deaths all at once.

—Yes, we should.

I said it almost too rationally. Susan came around the table, put her arms around me, and kissed me gently on the forehead. Anyone watching would have determined the whole story:

Two people meet. They have a wonderful affair but all good things come to an end. They part ways in a public place. To avoid a noisy breakup. No words necessary for this story. It's all in the body language. Mime. It didn't seem to matter to Susan now if anybody saw her in this obviously poignant moment. It was over, wasn't it? Nothing to gossip about now. Susan picked up her handbag along with the silver snuffbox.

—Phillip, I'm probably going to go away for a little while. Sort this out in my head. I'll be back.

Now I was really confused. What was there to sort out? What the fuck was there to sort out? She wasn't leaving James and it was over. *It* being us. We were over. But before I could make that point, she was gone.

Sherry was leaning against the rustic pine sideboard next to the kitchen door. The restaurant kept knives and forks in its huge old drawers. Water jugs lined up like soldiers on its top. Sherry had been the silent witness. The one who had determined the whole story. She looked genuinely forlorn. As if sorry the exchange between us had taken place—that she knew I was rude to her because I was hurting. She read all of that into Susan's gentle kiss on my head. The way Susan ran her fingers through my hair afterwards.

I felt sad.

Susan

I stepped out into the parking lot. I had made a proper mess of things. I thought it would be something we could discuss rationally.

I took a deep breath. Unfinished business.

I had asked Phillip to call me and maybe I shouldn't have. I shouldn't have said I was going to sort it out in my head either. Or that I'll be back—he may have thought I was opening the door again.

Messy as it was, he must surely have got the basic message though. Surely. And that was the point, wasn't it? Fuck it. I headed back to the shop.

Phillip

—Would you like some coffee?

—Yes, Sherry, that would be nice. I'll be right back. Would you bring me the check as well, please?

I got up and crossed the room. Most of the other diners had left the restaurant now. There was a man in the corner by himself reading his newspaper. The group of four ladies was quieter now, their exuberance worn out. They looked up at me, looked at each other, and bowed their heads in unison to avoid any further eye contact with me.

I pushed by empty tables that had the remnants of meals

still on them. There were deep red spots on the pink tablecloths—from the wine that was more carelessly poured towards the end of the meal. The silverware was gone except for a few desert forks and spoons. Still in their set position. Waiting patiently for deserts that were never ordered. Just coffee, please.

Olive-skinned bus boys hurried around; cleaning up the mess left by people they thought should have better manners.

Taking the step up to the bar area, I headed towards the men's room located in a corridor by the restaurant's entrance. I knew the restaurant's owner, David, quite well now. He was behind the bar reading a paper, enjoying a few peaceful moments before the early dinner crowd came in. He looked up and removed his reading glasses.

–Hello, Phillip.

–Hi, David. How are you? I'll be right back, I said unnecessarily. I waited a moment or two in the corridor while someone else finished in the bathroom. It was one of the kitchen staff. He smiled at me as he came out, still shaking his slightly wet hands. I always found it slightly disconcerting when an employee came out the loo in a restaurant where I had just eaten.

I went in and locked the door behind me. The bathroom was painted pale blue. The boy's version of the pink colors that dominated the restaurant's interior. I peed, zipped up, flushed and turned to the sink. I put one hand on either side of the basin, leaned down heavily on it, and looked down at the drain. I closed my eyes momentarily. I used to do this in bad old, good old days of drinking. To steady myself before heading back to the bar.

I examined my face in the mirror.

Tired, hungry and lonely are the three biggest triggers; the three things most likely to make an alcoholic pick up again. I wasn't tired. And I wasn't hungry, despite the fact that most of my lunch was left on the plate. But I did have this overwhelming sense of loneliness. Like I had just lost my best friend and I had, I suppose. I felt cut loose. Adrift. Empty.

Pull yourself together, Phillip. Phone your AA sponsor. Phone your darling sister. Jennifer would be good to talk to. See? You're not alone after all.

–Yes I am, I said quietly to myself. And I was.

I wandered back into the bar. David looked up again and went through the same motions of removing his glasses before speaking to me.

–How was your lunch today?

–Good, David, thank you. Good as always.

–Well that's nice to hear, Phillip. There are people who have been coming here for years and never actually say they've enjoyed the food. The chef goes nuts about it, but as I tell him, they keep coming back so they must like the smell coming from the kitchen.

Sherry popped her head into the bar.

–Shall I bring your coffee and check in here?

–That would be nice, Sherry. Thank you.

You would never know that she and I were mortal enemies just a little while ago.

I pulled out a stool from under the bar.

Sherry reappeared with the coffee and a black vinyl folder bearing the American Express logo. She put both down carefully on the bar.

–Whenever you're ready.

That's restaurant speak for *pay now because I want to go on my break* but I didn't take offense. Sherry was my new best friend. I took a sip of the coffee. It was very hot. Steaming. I set it to one side. David appeared to have said all he had to say for the moment and we lapsed into an easy silence as I paid the bill and he went back to reading his paper.

We were at the same bar, but in our own space.

I knew the feeling well. Drunks all bellied up to the mahogany. Real drunks, not just a group of people who have had a few too many. Drunks take their booze seriously. We lived for it. And we would die from it. I don't drink any more. But I don't drink any less either. Only we could save ourselves. You get sober when you're ready to get sober. And that normally means one final bout with the bottle. Hitting bottom as they say. C.S. Lewis decided that God allowed us to experience terrible lows in life in order to learn the lessons we wouldn't have otherwise learned. I had learned my lesson. I would never drink again. I had seen *lots of sad faces in lots of bad places* as the song goes.

I looked up and down the bar shelf. All the brands that I had once been so very acquainted with now looked strangely unfamiliar. A world I was out of touch with.

Like lasers though, my eyes focused on the *Calvados* bottle. *Eau de vie de cidre.* Water of life. Apple brandy. It was what I used to drink with my coffee. I could taste it. Before I could stop myself, the words tumbled out of my mouth. Along with an alcoholic's typical justification and lie.

–Hey, David. I don't have to work this afternoon, give me a *Calvados*, would you?

If he thought it, David didn't show any surprise at me ordering a drink. He was happy to serve me. He liked me.

–Of course, Phillip. It's on me. The first one anyway.

–Oh, there'll only be one.

Susan

I didn't go straight back to the shop but drove around for a while. I didn't want to have to deal with Phillip if he stopped by after lunch. I eventually returned about 4:30 but still felt a little apprehensive as I walked up the steps to the front door. When I opened up, the burglar alarm didn't give its usual warning beep. Didn't I activate it before I left for the restaurant? My mind had certainly been elsewhere—on what I was going to say to Phillip. I must be more careful. Robbers!

Phillip hadn't called—there was no voicemail at the shop. There was no sign that he had been there either, no nasty note on the front door. I would close again at 5:00 and get home to James. I wanted Phillip to call. But I didn't want him to call. Where was he?

Phillip

It is now 4.30. I have to leave. The words are echoing in my ears. Words I had heard over and over in AA meetings: One is too many, a thousand isn't enough. I throw crumpled bills down on the bar and turn to walk out. I bump into a table on the way. I am drunk. Very drunk. David pretends not to notice and simply tells me to take care. I pull the front door toward me instead of pushing it. Finally, it opens. I gulp the air outside like I'd been gulping *Calvados* all afternoon. Large mouthfuls. Anxious for an effect. An immediate reward. I lean back against the side of the restaurant. Where did I park my car? Did I bring the car? I closed my eyes and tried to concentrate. All that enters the fuzz is my miserable failure.

I had thrown it all away.

My precious sobriety gone.

First, I lose Susan. And now my mind.

Another fucking relapse.

I am angry now. This is all Susan's fault. I wouldn't have got drunk if she had stayed with me. If she hadn't left the restaurant, hadn't ended it. That bitch.

I want to get down on my knees.

–Help me, God. Please.

I see the car. Where I left it, of course. Carefully parked when I was sober earlier. Happier times. I straighten up, hold myself rigid and try to walk as normally as I can. I don't fumble for my keys but miraculously go to the right pocket first time. I close one eye in a vain attempt to focus and try to push the unlock button. I can't hold the fob steady and I drop the keys. They disappear from view. Where the fuck did they go? I am swaying as I look down to the ground. If I can't see my keys, the ones I had in my hands two seconds ago, I can't drive. This much dawns on me. I am lucid for a brief moment. I leave the car where it is and walk across the parking lot to the street.

Susan had said to call her. I did but she wasn't there. I left her a message. David had let me use the phone on the bar but walked away when he heard me. I thought I was talking quietly and discreetly but maybe I was shouting, just like those four women earlier.

I decide I should go to *Remains To Be Seen*. Get her to see some sense. Leave James. Live with me. Just as we planned. Just as I *thought* we had planned.

I walk across the village green and past the post office. Some firemen were outside the tiny volunteer firehouse chatting and polishing equipment. They glance quickly at me. I must look drunk. I stagger past the library and the Old Woodford Museum and Historical Society.

I'm at the village church. Something makes me go in. Sit in a pew, sober up a bit.

I've always admired the church from the outside but I'd never been in.

It was New England Gothic. I push open the heavy front doors and step into a dark vestibule. I have to adjust my eyes. Which is a bit of a joke right now. I go through the next set of doors and into the church itself. The ornately carved wood details in the ceiling are magnificent. I can still appreciate this, drunk as I am. There are a dozen or so pews on either side of a broad aisle. The pews are painted white with walnut trim. Deep red cushions soften the seats. It occurs to me that the cushions are in place for the privileged tushes of Old Woodford's elite. Why should they park their upper-class arses on hard wood when praising God? Look at the size of the pledge they made last Advent! Comfort and Joy with the emphasis on comfort. That's what these upstanding, sitting down, citizens deserve.

Stained glass windows in Gothic style frames line the long walls of the church. Five on either side. The first, the one closest to the chancel, is predominately blue. Then green, yellow, red, and purple. They are beautiful. A group of five or six people are sitting in the choir seats. They look over at me but then turn back to their business. I slide into a pew. I close one eye to try to focus better. I'm rat-arsed.

A, O, U.

I have stumbled into choir practice. The little group is being led by a woman whose features I can't quite make out—she is in half-profile at the piano facing her singers. Her blonde hair is pulled back but some strands have come loose in an appealing way. First, she stands and plays, then sits down heavily on the piano stool. She is obviously serious about her business. She tucks one foot underneath like a child sitting on a sofa watching TV, and pumps away at the piano pedal with the other. She is playing with only one hand and waving the other at her rapt group. She is dressed casually—a baggy shirt that is tailored enough to tell you it was designed for a woman and not a man. She wears it loose over black leggings.

A, O, U.

I am examining the choir one by one. The men are seated in the third row. A curly-haired man wearing glasses glances up at me and then back to the blonde lady. He sneaks another look but catches me staring at him and turns away again. Next to him is a short little man (he only comes up to Curly's shoulders) with a pleasant face. His silver hair is brushed away from his forehead and he is wearing heavy, black-rimmed glasses. For some reason, Buddy Holly's spectacles come to mind. He has a good nose that sits on a bushy, silver moustache. He is earnest and serious. To his left is a white-haired Santa Claus. This guy is a ringer for Father Christmas. It occurs to me that it is pretty smart of the church to hire its own St. Nicholas.

A, O, U.

In front of the curly-headed man is a black woman. Even from this distance and despite my altered state of mind, I see she has delicate skin, slightly freckled. She stares intently at her leader. This is an eclectic group but obviously with a common purpose.

A, O, U.

I realize now what I am listening to, what they are singing. The musical vowels. Over and over. Suddenly the blonde piano player barks out with a passion that takes me by surprise. I jump in my seat, almost as if she is reprimanding me.

–Again. Again. I am not going to stop until I hear what I need to hear.

I straighten up. Her words are meant for the choir, but they have caught my attention as well: *I am not going to stop until I hear what I need to hear.*

She gets up from the piano and goes over to the singers. She puts both hands on the railing that separates the choir seats from the rest of the chancel and leans forward. She shouts and laughs at the same time. She fakes exasperation and repeats herself.

–I am not going to stop until I hear what I need to hear.

She doesn't bother going back to the piano this time, but sings out loudly where she is standing. She turns her palms over and raises her hands heavenwards in time with her rising, powerful crescendo. She belts out the musical vowels and the choir joins her enthusiastically. They have woken up. They've got it. By jove, they've got it.

A—Ah,

O—Oh,

U—Oooo!

I stand up and shouted.

–Thank you. Thank you, choir. Thank you, Blondie.

They stop in mid-crescendo. They look panic stricken. Totally alarmed. A nut job in their midst. Their collective faces go white. Do I have a gun? Was I going to go on a rampage?

But all I harm is myself. I bang into the end of the pew as I tried to round it too quickly.

There would be a bruise.

But at least I knew what I was going to say to Susan now.

Susan

I knew he was drunk the moment I saw him coming up the steps to the shop.

The steps he used to spring up in anticipation of seeing me.

Now it was the classic one step forward, two back. Like a cartoon. His beautiful face was red and bloated. This just from one afternoon's drinking.

He obviously had stirred up all the old stuff. Oh, Phillip.

I would hide in the *Ha-Ha* cupboard. I tried to lock the door but the bolt I had drawn a million times for some inexplicable reason wouldn't budge.

–Shit. Fuck. Shit. Shit. Fuck.

Phillip got to the door faster than I thought and there was no point in trying to hide now—he had seen me. I opened the door and let him in. Better to have him inside than a scene out on the street.

–Hi, I was just closing up.

He totally ignored me. This was a Phillip I had never seen. He blurted out:

–I am not going to stop until I hear what I need to hear.

–I beg your pardon, Phillip.

–I am not going to stop until I hear what I need to hear, Susan.

He spat out *Susan* sarcastically, as an echo of the way I had said, *Phillip*. I answered him firmly now.

–And what do you want to hear, Phillip?

My controlling tone didn't work this time. He started screaming at me.

–You know what I want to fucking hear you fucking conniving fucking bitch.

He didn't pause between words. Still shouting, he came around the table in the middle of the shop—the table we had fucked on—and bumped clumsily against it. All the china and bric-a-brac wobbled precariously but without falling over. Then as he stepped toward me, his foot caught the leg supporting the drop leaf. He staggered back trying to gain his balance by grabbing the edge of the table but slipped to the floor and collapsed in an inebriated heap taking all the china and bric-a-brac with him. Amazingly, he sprang to his feet again, like a cat. I'd seen drunks do that before. Man down! No, hold on a sec—man back up again. His verbal assault didn't miss a beat either.

–Let me fucking well tell you something, Mrs...*Mrs. Birley* that is.

He had never called me that before.

–Mr. Birley is going to find out all about this. He'll get all the sordid details whether he likes it or not. And I don't think he will like the details, Mrs. Or does he already know how you like to eat dick for main course and pussy for desert? You fucking bitch. And Sarah. I'll tell James all about Sarah. How do you think he'll feel when he finds out he's been keeping your sapphic sidekick under the family roof all these years? Eh? What do you think he'll think about that, Mrs. Birley?

I was suddenly scared for the first time. He was right. I'd led him on. Led him into bed. Allowed him to fall in love with me. But so fucking what? He was a big boy. He didn't have to fall in love with me.

–First you love me. Then you don't. I don't know where I fucking stand, Susan.

He was jumping from one rant to another.

I put my hands over my ears. I needed to stop the madness. And so I looked up at him. I made the eyes that he loved. I even brought a tear to them.

–Okay, okay, Phillip. No more shouting. No more fighting. I'll do it.

This actually calmed him down. The shouting stopped. His rapid breathing slowed. The threatening looks gone.

I was back in control.

I could smell the stale booze on his breath. He smiled now. Jekyll and Hyde. I had lied to him, of course, but I think he believed me. He was hearing what he wanted to hear. That I would leave James and ask for a divorce.

I knew he suddenly wanted me, right at that moment, and so I did what I do best.

I took his hand and led him through to the back of the shop and pulled him towards the Edwardian sofa.

The sofa where we had made love so many times. Where we had sometimes simply fucked. Where he turned me over. And slapped me.

Doing things to me that James probably didn't even know could be done. Things that I didn't know could be done.

I unbuttoned his shirt. Loosened his belt. Slid my hands inside his pants. Taking care to kiss him as lovingly as always.

I would miss him.

I would miss his beautiful cock. The way I sat on top of him. Feeling him like a laser, penetrating me. Stroking his balls. Sucking him. An act that turned me on as much as him. Sometimes, I would suck him until he fell asleep. I loved the way he just shrank in my mouth. I would feel him go limp. All over. And then he was gone, into a deep slumber.

Now I raised my skirt up over my hips. I wasn't wearing any panties. He liked me that way. And I'd gotten used to it. I liked the feeling of soft, silky skirts or dresses cold against my buttocks. I undid my blouse. Just enough for him to kiss the tops of my breasts.

I didn't want to be completely naked for this.

And he wouldn't think anything of it. He liked me half undressed. We had played games where he pretended to force me. Getting at me through my clothes. That's right, it was a game of rape. Using his full strength against me. And I liked it. I really liked it.

We played it for the first time when we were in Newport. I lay in the dark room and he went outside to the balcony. He pretended to be an intruder. I heard the door creak open. I was scared for a moment. I heard him come into the room.

Stealthily. He was almost too good at this. Suddenly, his hand was over my mouth. I tried to sit up. He pushed me back down. I tried to scream. He pressed down with his hands on my lips even harder.

I felt him tugging at my clothes. And then suddenly, he was kissing me gently. He was Phillip again.

—*Shhh,* Susan. It's me. I'm back.

And then we made love. Sweet gentle love. A total contradiction to everything that had happened a few moments earlier.

A contradiction.

Just like our relationship now. I started out by loving the idea of him. He just wanted an affair. Now all I wanted was the affair and nothing else. Certainly not leaving my dear, sweet husband. But Phillip was in love with me and wanted this to be more. And it couldn't, it just couldn't.

I would have to end it.

I lay down on the sofa and opened my legs. He was already down on his knees.

His tongue found me; I was as wet as ever for him. I couldn't understand it, thinking what I thinking, what I was about to do.

And yet, wet. Full of desire. Want. Need.

It must be adrenaline. That's right. Not desire or want or need. Just pure adrenaline.

Oh, god.

He was taking soft bites of my thighs now, working all the way up my body until he was finally kissing my lips. I tasted myself. How could he have uttered such terrible things to me earlier? How could such angry words have passed his gentle mouth?

He slid one finger inside me. Then two. And then suddenly, his cock.

His beautiful cock.

I leaned back, my head over the edge of the sofa, and I reached for one of the candlesticks. The Georgian candlesticks he so adored. Sheffield. 1799. John Green,

Silversmith. The candlesticks bought with love for Phillip just a few months but now a lifetime ago. He insisted on keeping them in the shop, on the table near the sofa, so they'd be within easy reach when we were making love. On display but with a *Not for Sale* sign. And then he would enjoy me scratching his back with the edge of the sharp base. Almost drawing blood. Almost but not quite. Leaving marks certainly.

My hand went around his back. I held the candlestick by the column and gently let the heavy base down on his spine. And then I pulled it up. Up his back. Between his shoulder blades. Scratching him deeply.

I could feel that he was about to come.

He said the candlesticks turned him on more than anything. The sharp, sudden pain that I inflicted. He wanted more.

–Keep doing it, he whispered. I caught the stale booze again and turned my head to one side.

I scratched deeper. Harder. His back shrank away from the stick. He got harder inside me. He pushed deeper into me. I could feel him coming. I was coming.

How could I be at a time like this? But I was. I didn't care why. It was all happening at once. A frenzy. An ecstasy. I shouted out.

–Ohhhhhhhhhh, my god.

I raised the candlestick as high as my arm would reach. Above his head. He wasn't going to tell James anything. James would never know about Sarah. Never. I'll make sure of that.

I caught sight of the inscription on the base of the candlestick. It was telling me to do it. Urging me on.

–*Honi soit qui mal y pense*, I screamed out. –Fucking evil on him who thinks fucking evil!

I brought the candlestick down. Hard.

But then.

Fuck! No! Not murder, Susan. Not over this. As horrible as it's been. Not murder. At the last second, I let the candlestick slip from my grip but it still caught the edge of his shoulder and clattered heavily to the floor. A split second later he cried out.

—Arrrggghhh!

His full weight collapsed on me. First the cry and then he crumpled. Just as he always did when he came. The air went out of him. I put my arms around him. A trickle of sweat rolled down his back. I followed its trail with my forefinger but when I looked at my hand over his shoulder, I saw blood. Maybe I had gone deep when I scratched him. Maybe the candlestick had cut into his shoulder. Instinctively, I asked him what I always asked him.

—Was that good, baby?

He didn't answer.

—Baby?

I let my fingers run through his hair, tugging on it. His hair was wet. Sticky.

I looked at my hand again. Bright red. More blood.

I got scared.

I tried to turn my head. I tried to push Phillip to one side.

I was panicking. Gasping for air. I couldn't see the candlestick on the floor. It wasn't where it had fallen.

And then, shoes. Beautifully polished. Church's English Shoes. Hand-made.

Beautifully tailored trousers breaking perfectly over the shoes. Savile Row. Bespoke tailors.

With a final shove, I was able to push Phillip over.

Enough to see. Enough to look up.

He was standing there looking down at me.

His arms by his side.

The candlestick was in his left hand. Hanging down by his thigh.

There was blood on it. Blood. Yes, it was blood.

My eyes didn't need to look up but they did.

And they met his.

Wide. Paralyzed. Full of fear.

James.

My dear, sweet James.

James looked at me momentarily, tears welled up in his eyes, and then he looked away. A hand went to his shoulder. A hand I recognized. A hand that had touched me. Caressed me.

She stepped forward from behind James. She raised her other hand to her chest. A candlestick was clasped in it. The second of the pair. There was blood all over her blue silk blouse. Red and blue and the white of her pearl necklace. Red, white and blue. Oh, my god.

Not Sarah as well. Not my darling Sarah.

Jennifer

—Ouch.

—What? What I have done, darling?

—Nothing. Nothing. It's not you, Sandy.

—What then, Jennifer? Didn't you like the way I was kissing you?

Her long legs were either side of my face. Her small tight arse was perched above my chest, her head was face down between my thighs. Her hands were playing games on the inside of my calves.

—I love the way you kiss me down there. It's just that I suddenly got this sharp pain in the back of my head. And then a feeling like someone had pulled my hair.

—Let me rub it for you.

Sandy rolled off me. Next thing I knew, the back of my head was being massaged.

—Oh, Sandy, I love you.

—And I love you, Jen. I really do.

Now Sandy was kissing my neck. My shoulders. Hands over my breasts. She loved my breasts. Small. Firm. Tapering to almost invisible nipples.

And I loved her breasts.

A complete contrast to mine. Sandy had big, beautiful

boobs. Rubens would have loved them.

Her tan marks ended where the sun wasn't allowed. But where I was. Making me privy to wonderful white hills; snow-covered mountains. I needed both hands to cup just one breast.

Sandy was a magnificent woman. Like the Hollywood stars of old. The days of real women like Jane Russell.

Her mother had been an actress in fifties and sixties; one of the girls with impossible figures that followed the male movie star around while he was strumming on his guitar and singing love songs in unlikely public settings. All in Technicolor!

And Sandy inherited that body. I loved shopping with Sandy and watching the double takes she got from men. Or sitting with her in a meeting and watching the blokes talking to her breasts instead of making eye contact with her.

Once, after I had come out, I introduced her to my boss. And all he could say afterwards was:

–So what are they like? Are they fantastic? I bet they are.

It gave me a feeling of power.

Knowing that the men were wondering what she was like in bed, what her tits would be like out, all the while knowing I was the one she was going to sleep with that night.

My journey off into the peaks and valleys of Sandy's boobs had diverted my attention from the pain that was still hammering away at the back of my head.

–I'm going to get a Tylenol, Sandy.

–Shall I get it for you?

–No, Sandy. I'm good. I walked into the bathroom off the bedroom.

We had just moved into a hacienda on Hayworth in West Hollywood. It was a nice house. A porn star had apparently lived there once.

–We can play games of deep throat without the dicks, said Sandy merrily to the real estate agent who showed us around.

—We'll use our tongues, I chimed in, just to be shocking.

I went to the cabinet behind the bathroom mirror. As I swung the door open, I caught sight of my face. I'd just had my hair cut. Boy's length. Suddenly it seemed I was staring at Phillip. It scared me. I went cold. The pain in my head hit again. This time harder. I grabbed my neck and closed my eyes.

—Ouch. Ouch.

Then I looked up slowly at my reflection in the mirror.

—Phillip. Are you all right, Phillip?

My stomach lurched and a nervous, empty feeling swept over me. All my nerve endings sparked at once.

My twin was in danger.

I just knew it. Oh, Christ. Was he drinking again? Had he fallen over drunk and banged his head? Was that the pain I was feeling? My mum's voice echoed through my mind: *Phillip fell off his bike when he was a boy and you cried from the pain!*

Four in the afternoon here. Seven in the evening in New York. I dashed through the bedroom and into the living room. I grabbed the phone and called him. Four rings and then Phillip's voice.

—Hello? How are you doing?

—Phillip! Are you all right?

—*BEEEEEEP.*

The fucking answering machine. Phillip had recorded it to sound like he was really answering. It drove me nuts. The number of one-sided conversations I had started before the beep kicked in.

—Phillip, it's Jen. It's late afternoon. Early evening. Whatever. Call me, darling. I need to hear your voice. Your live voice. Not this stupid answering machine. And by the way, please change your message otherwise I won't tell you any stories about Sandy's tits.

I put the phone down and hesitated by it. Something was wrong. I could feel it.

—What was that about my tits? Sandy called from the bedroom.

I turned toward her voice and she was standing there, framed in the doorway. Totally naked. I had trimmed her bush so low, sometimes it looked like she had no pubic hair at all. I had shaved her pussy to match mine.

–Where did you learn to trim your bush so nice and neatly? Sandy had asked as I was shaving her.

–My brother.

Sandy said nothing but digested this answer and seemed to enjoy the very notion of it.

She leaned against the doorframe. Her right hand went up to her left breast. She slowly spread her fingers and massaged in circular motions until her nipple went hard. She licked the end of her left forefinger and delicately placed it on the nipple on her right breast. I felt myself go wet.

She cupped both hands under her magnificent breasts and pushed them up. Then she raised her hands over her head. She ran her fingers through her hair. My hand went to my clitoris. I'd seen her do this a million times, unashamedly exhibiting her chest, but each time felt like the first time. My clit was standing straight up, like a man's erect cock. I just barely touched it and felt my knees start to buckle. Sandy turned and faced the bedroom. Her long body was silhouetted against the light. Her hands now went down to her buttocks. She used the same circular motion on her arse, like a stripper in front of an audience of raucous men waving five-dollar bills. Oh, my god, Sandy. She spread her legs and I could see where her pubic hair, the pubes I hadn't trimmed, hung down between her legs. Like a young boy's attempt at a beard. She looked over her shoulder at me, then at the bed, and then back at me.

–Coming? she asked.

I could barely answer. I already was.

–Sandy, wait.

Sandy stopped in the doorway. She turned back to me. Her left hand went to the doorframe. She rested her right hand on her right hip, pushing her left hip up slightly. She was so sexy. I stepped forward and took her hand. I pulled her all the way around. She immediately pushed her body into mine. I turned my head to the left. She turned hers to her left. Our lips met in the middle. Her tongue went straight into my mouth. Her smell, her unique smell filling my senses. She dipped her knees slightly and as she raised herself up again, her pelvic bone crashed and banged against mine. Not soft and feminine. But hard and hungry. Her hands slipped down over my arse. She pulled at my buttocks. I squeezed my cheeks together. They were hard in her hands. Like a little boy's, she had said once. I ran my hands up her back and covered her shoulder blades. Then I pulled her hard into my chest. She put her arms all the way around me and squeezed me tight around the waist. Lifting me off the ground slightly. She pushed me back. Like she was forcing my body into a tight space. It hurt. Oh, god. No.

I pushed her back. A little too forcefully. Her shoulder hit the doorframe.

–Jennifer!

–I'm sorry, Sandy, I'm so sorry. It's Phillip. He's been hurt. He's being pushed and shoved around. I just know it. I can feel it. Sandy, I can't do this now.

I turned and practically ran back to the living room—to the laptop sitting on the coffee table. I threw off the magazines and newspapers that were covering the keyboard. *Vanity Fair, Vogue, The Hollywood Reporter.* Where I had carelessly dropped them when I came home. I was in a hurry because Sandy wanted me straight away.

It was late afternoon now but I could still get the red-eye. It left at 9:00 and arrived in New York before 6:00 in the morning. Working in film production, I did it all the time. Booking at the last minute. Getting Ronnie into New York for a sudden meeting with the studio brass at 8:00 in the morning. A few hours later, he was on the 11:00 flight back to L.A. in time for a 5:00 casting session the same afternoon. The time difference working in our favor. And always first class. Big seats so there was sleep to be had. I retrieved the Paramount Pictures travel agent's number from my computer address book. The studio where Ronnie's latest feature was in development. I switched emotional gears. I needed co-operation. I grabbed the phone again and dialed furiously.

–Hi, Steven. Stevie baby.

–Okay, Jen. What is it now? What do you want?

Steve was great. Bent as a nine-quid note as we'd say in England, but he was great.

–I have a problem. I need to get on the red eye to New York tonight. I need to see my brother.

–Is he good-looking?

–He's my twin. A male version of me.

–Hmmm. That could work. Just a sec, darling.

I heard Steve pick up another phone. A few minutes later, I heard kissy, kissy in the background.

–Here you go, Jennifer, my dear. You owe me big time. I had to promise my body to American Airlines. Flight 10. Seat 2A. You're all set. Between us girls, I'm putting this down as *Wardrobe and fittings for New York cast*.

–I love you, Steve. Thanks. Thanks. Thanks.

I turned back to the bedroom to see my gorgeous Sandy packing an overnight bag for me. She had switched on *The Weather Channel*. She glanced at the TV and then looked at me.

–I figured you'd want to go light. No waiting around for checked luggage at that ungodly hour in the morning. You'll need a raincoat though. It's apparently going to be wet all day tomorrow. And I've thrown a pair of my knickers in, just so you don't forget me.

–I love you, Sandy.

–I love you, Jen.

–Thanks for understanding.

–I'm not sure I do understand. But your sixth sense or whatever it is you share with Phillip seems to be in overdrive. You won't be happy until you see his face, see him safe and sound.

Susan

James lifted up the candlestick and silently examined it, not believing what had just happened. Sarah seemed to go into shock. All the blood had drained from her already white face. She started breathing rapidly—like she couldn't control herself—and then she let out great big sobs. Choking for air.

—Help me, I said, quietly at first.

James continued to stare at the bloodied candlestick.

—What have I done? Jesus, what have I done?

Sarah suddenly stopped sobbing and looked at the candlestick that was in her hand. She put it carefully back on the table beside the sofa, treating it with reverence, as if it had a life of its own.

—Me, James. It was me who hit him.

—Then we both did it, Sarah.

For God's sake. This was like something out of a black comedy. The two of them claiming killing rights. Now I screamed.

—SARAH! JAMES! Get him the fuck off me.

James stepped forward and pulled at Phillip's shoulders. There was no resistance of course, and Phillip immediately flipped over. His glassy eyes seemed to be staring at us all. It scared the shit out of Sarah. James stumbled back and Phillip fell to the floor. I sat up gasping for air. My hands were covered in blood. There was also matted hair on my fingertips. I must have pulled it out in the struggle to free myself. Phillip's shirtfront was stained red where I had tried to push him off. Broken china and bric-a-brac was scattered over the floor. The drop leaf table was half up, half down. The area rug was bunched in one corner. I waited a second, and then I spoke. And I said the most ridiculous thing.

—It's all right.

If Phillip had been with us, he would have said:

—Not for me it ain't, mate.

I stood on unsteady legs and straightened my clothing. I

needed to think. James watched me adjust my skirt and then turned to the shop window, staring out into the gathering darkness of the evening.

–He was raping you, Susan. I hit him with the candlestick. He was raping you.

Sarah made a gesture for me not to say anything. She turned to James.

–Yes, that's right, James.

James looked away from the window and back to me.

–Susan, we must call the police.

–No, James.

Sarah grabbed his arm and shook him. As if trying to shake him out of his shock.

–No, James. Just sit.

James collapsed into the wingback chair. I looked down at Phillip. His jaw had dropped open. His eyes were seeing nothing. But he was still beautiful.

James

I knew all about it. The affair. And this is going to sound pathetic, but I truly mean it. If it was going to make Susan happy, so be it.

I clearly wasn't making her happy.

Maybe she would have her little fling, get it out of her system, and then we could move on. That was all right by me. Better than the alternative. A divorce. Having to tell all our friends and family. Dividing everything up after all these years. Bickering over money. Giving most of it to fucking lawyers.

No, I didn't want that. And I don't think she did either.

I chose to ignore the obvious. Her sliding away for the afternoon. Telling me she was doing inventory with Sarah. All very careless really. It only took one call to the shop to find out she wasn't there. The perfume. Suddenly having a bikini wax or whatever it is called when you trim up down there. I saw her reflection in the mirror as she was getting dressed one day. It rather shocked me.

The bedroom door being shut in the middle of the day and Susan whispering on the phone. And then closing her eyes on the one occasion we made love over the last three months and calling me Phillip.

I heard the phone messages on the plane. And then the fuss over the silly fax at the *Danube*. It didn't take long to establish that Sarah hadn't sent it. Sarah gave it away without even saying so.

And when I slipped twenty euros to Jerome, that prick of a night porter, he could practically recite the bastard's poem to me. He revealed more details from the fax than I actually wanted. It explained the phone call on the balcony the night before though. Pretending she had to speak to a client in New York. After thirty years, a chap knows what his wife's heavy breathing means. Knows that a certain kind of panting doesn't come about because his wife has just run a marathon around the *City of Lights*. No, this was panting stimulated by the pant load that was now in a heap on the floor.

She could have her affair as long as it was discreet.

But it had gone public, and that was when I felt the shame. Not shame that Susan was having an affair. Shame that I wasn't keeping the home fires burning. I don't know. Maybe my upbringing. An Army life. It seemed that I had failed and that hurt me. What would the other chaps say?

The final straw came this afternoon—the phone calls. The first from Hubert.

—Is Susan all right, James?

—As far as I know, Hubert. Why do you ask?

—I was at *Bistro Bijoux* having a spot of lunch, catching up on the newspapers, and she practically flew out of the restaurant. She seemed terribly upset. She didn't even acknowledge my hello. I'm not sure she even saw me, James. She was in that much of a hurry.

—Who was she with?

—Don't know. Maybe a customer. She had brought a bit

of silver with her. I saw her put it down on the table. It looked like a little box of some sort. He was examining it.

–He? It was a male customer?

–Yes, a man.

–Thanks, Hubert. I'm sure she's fine. I'll call you back or see you at the club next week.

–Yes. Yes. I hope I haven't said anything to upset you?

–Not at all. I'm glad you're being a good friend. Thank you.

I had no sooner put the phone down than it rang again.

–James, it's Monica.

I hated Monica. She was one of the gossipy ladies that do lunch club.

Even Susan questioned why she had maintained a friendship with her over the years.

Susan called her *Radio Monica.*

If you wanted something to get around town quickly, simply call Monica, tell her about it, and then swear her to secrecy. Next thing, it would be on the front page of the *Woodford Wag.*

–Hello, Monica.

I didn't want to get into a conversation with her so I continued to speak over the top of her.

–Susan's not here. I'll tell her you called.

–Thank you. But don't hang up, James. I just wanted to apologize for not inviting her over to our table lunchtime. We were having a party at *Bistro Bijoux* for one of the girls. You know how we do. Susan seemed very wrapped up with her lunch partner. A man. I didn't want to interrupt. I'm not sure she even saw me.

–I'll send your apologies, Monica.

I hung up. Susan was getting sloppy. Seen by two people in the same restaurant and she didn't see them. Eyes only for her *customer* apparently.

I sat down and thought for a while. It would have to stop. Sarah must know about it. She knew Susan better than anyone. Even better than I did.

Sarah

When James called, I was caught off guard. I don't like that. Susan doesn't have an obligation to tell me everything but if she was having public tiffs with her lover, there's not much I can do to protect her. And I wasn't going to spin some whopper to James. I felt bad enough as it was covering up while Susan was away shagging Phillip in Newport.

James never ever knew or suspected anything about my own relationship with Susan. And that was a guilt I lived with for many years. I never got over Susan. When MKT transferred me to New York, I was embarrassed when James suggested I move into the guesthouse on their property. But Susan insisted it was a great idea. Between us girls. Between friends. And that's how it had stayed all these years.

Now James wanted to know about Phillip. Was Susan going to leave him?

I told James I was pretty certain she would not leave. That this just was a fling, that it would be short-lived.

He wanted to know how long it had been going on.

–Phillip first came into the shop a few weeks before Thanksgiving last year, I told him. –But I don't believe the affair started until late January.

It was now the end of March and so it had been going on less than three months. That seemed to comfort James. He said something about letting her get it out of her system but that the affair couldn't be public. He needed to confront her and stop it. He asked me to go over to the main house. When I walked in, he was dressed ready to go out. Typical James. Shirt and tie. Blazer. Polished shoes.

–I'm going to the shop, Sarah. I just tried to call, but there was no answer. I didn't leave a message. Please come with me, Sarah. I want her to see this isn't about a husband slamming her for an indiscretion, but about the two people who love her most. Simply caring for her. Wanting her to see sense.

James needed me. That much I could see. I agreed to go with him. It was 3:45. We'd be at the shop just after 4:00.

James

When we arrived at the shop, Susan wasn't there. Sarah opened up. I didn't have a key; the shop was Susan's. It was her domain. Sarah turned off the burglar alarm and we went in. The voicemail light was blinking on the phone. We played the message several times before we could understand what was being said. Sarah turned to me.

–It's Phillip. He's drunk.

–He sounded very threatening, Sarah.

–Yes. This seems to be very out of character from what little I know of him.

Sarah obviously didn't want me to think that she knew Phillip well. That she was party to this affair. She frowned.

–Sarah, what is it? Tell me.

–Phillip's an alcoholic. Susan told me. I'm sorry, but that's part of the reason I don't think Susan would leave you, James. As much as Susan has enjoyed this *fling*, she wouldn't consider Phillip marriage material because of his past. That it wouldn't be quite proper to introduce him to the kind of people she has in her life. Despite the fact he's been sober for eleven months. Well he was. He's clearly drunk now. And it sounds like he's heading this way. To have it out, as he put it. Make her see sense. I guess we're all trying to make Susan see sense today, James.

I managed to force a smile. I normally have good instincts about what to do in difficult situations but I was confused now. On the one hand I wanted to make sure Susan was safe. But I also wanted this to end. If Phillip was coming over to have it out, then maybe I should just let that take its course. And if Sarah was right, the simple fact Phillip had started drinking again would be more reason than ever to end the affair. There was clearly no future in it.

–I wish I could be here, but not be here, Sarah. Be ready

to protect Susan, but let her deal with Phillip and end this once and for all.

Sarah went to the front door, locked it with her key from the inside but didn't slide the bolt across. The door could still be unlocked and opened from the outside. She walked back to the wall at the rear of the shop.

—You can have your wish, James. Come over here.

Sarah

We stepped inside the *Ha-Ha* cupboard and I pulled the door shut. Susan would notice the burglar alarm was turned off but that didn't seem to matter right now. We were here to protect her. James wasn't surprised by this hidden space. He said he had seen this kind of thing before. In the IRA houses they raided in Northern Ireland. I could feel his anxiety in the dark but he said nothing. We waited; there was only the sound of our breathing. I had erased Phillip's message from the machine. There was no need for Susan to hear the language he was using. The threats he was making. We were here now and we would simply appear, seemingly out of nowhere, if things got ugly. We had prepared ourselves for a nasty argument though. Phillip's message had already promised that. We heard Susan come into the shop. A little while later, there was a scramble by the front door. And then the obvious sound of a table being knocked over. We heard Phillip screaming at Susan. James wanted to go out then, but I held him back. And then it went quiet. Susan was speaking softly and gently. We heard the unmistakable sounds of lovemaking. Or fucking. Or shagging. Or whatever it was that Susan and Phillip called it. But then Susan cried out—it was that cry of hers that was so familiar to me. But James heard only danger.

—He's raping her!

He pushed open the door. Susan was underneath Phillip. Half-naked. Phillip was fucking her furiously. A candlestick was on the floor; one of the heavy Georgian's with the *Not for Sale* sign. James got to it in a flash. I grabbed the other candlestick—the one still sitting on the table at the edge of the sofa. I came from the left. *Left is deaf,* Susan had told me once about Phillip's deafness in one ear. James came from behind. Phillip didn't hear us. He didn't hear a thing.

James

Name. Rank. Serial Number. Army training. I know how to stick to a story. You gave as few details as possible. Even under interrogation. I know about interrogation. I know about being locked up in small spaces. I know what it can do to a chap. The isolation you endure never leaves you. It becomes a mindset that stays with you all your life. You get to actually enjoy being by yourself. Being left alone. I'd served in Belfast in the seventies. Undercover. Infiltration. My cover was blown but that was almost a relief. I was conflicted about the fighting from the start. Like I was attacking my own. Ireland was my second home.

I'd never waver from the story line:

–I thought he was a robber who had broken into the shop. He had gone on a rampage. Breaking everything. He was raping my wife. I came up behind him. I told him to stop but he didn't respond. Either ignoring me or not hearing me. I hit him twice with a candlestick. Sarah was only holding the other one for self-defense. End of story. Name. Rank. Serial Number.

Sarah

I saw Susan's face when she was underneath Phillip and all I could do was sob.

I knew that look. She had climaxed.

She had *come* in the middle of all this.

How could she?

A wave of anger and shame swept over me. I thought I was going to be sick.

Susan

I glanced over at Sarah. She had started to pick up the broken china, ignoring the fact that Phillip was motionless next to her on the floor.

—Leave it, I said sharply.

Sarah looked up startled.

I went over to a shelf that was full of more bric-a-brac. Junky stuff that just added ambience to the shop. I raised my right arm across my chest as far as it would go and whipped the back of my hand along the front of the shelf. China and glass and silver crashed into each and tumbled like dominoes before sliding off the far end of the shelf and landing in a broken heap on the floor. I stepped over the mess and took big strides over to a second shelf display. It was filled with faux antique Christmas ornaments. I left them out all year round. It never ceased to amaze me that people would come in the shop in the middle of the summer, dressed in shorts, and buy something for their next Christmas tree. Well, see you next year, ornaments. This time I used my left arm and gave the decorations a good backhanded slap. I took down one of the mirrors and threw that on the floor and stepped on it for good measure.

I felt demonic now.

—Seven years bad luck. Fuck you!

I turned back to Sarah and James. They were wide-eyed.

—Not just a rape, James, I screamed. —A robbery. Help me with Phillip.

Sarah got large black garbage bags from the basement. I managed to prop up Phillip's top half while Sarah slipped a bag over his head and shoulders and pulled it down to his waist. I stumbled around to Phillip's feet. I stood astride Phillip and lifted up his legs. Sarah pulled a bag over his feet, up under the backs of his legs, and brought it up to meet the bag that was covering Phillip's top.

We interlaced the two separate drawstrings creating the impression of a black body bag with a snazzy yellow belt.

Sarah got string and we trussed his arms and legs tightly over the top of the plastic. Phillip had tied *me* up once. But that was then.

–Okay, James. We need you.

Sarah had already figured out the next move. She went over to the *Ha-Ha* cupboard. The door was ajar and she opened it all the way.

I told James to pick up Phillip by the middle. Get the center of gravity. James stumbled as he lifted him from the ground. He squeezed Phillip around the waist and took hesitant steps towards the cupboard. He dumped him in. Pushing and shoving at the black bag until it was squeezed into the tight space. He stood back. Breathing hard. Sarah looked at me. I nodded. She pushed the door shut. It disappeared into the wall. Just as Phillip had said, you'd never know it was there.

The floor was highly polished and the blood from Phillip's head wiped up easily. Apart from that, it was a reverse clean up. I opened the safe and took out the rest of the silver collection I had amassed for Phillip. I took down the valuable paintings and mirrors that needed to be kept. I separated the solid silver pieces from the silver-plate. The good china from the reproductions. These robbers knew what they were looking for. Sarah got more garbage bags and shipping boxes from the basement and everything we were taking with us went into them. The big furniture stayed. We left the table with one leaf up and the other down. It looked in suitable disarray. We took several trips down the stairs and through the basement until the Range Rover was full. The back seats were still flat from where Phillip and I had fucked in it a few days before. We were able to lay all the paintings and the mirrors in the cavernous space. I covered everything with the same blanket that had covered us while we were shagging.

James and Sarah slipped across the street to the cinema parking lot; they took more boxes and bags with them. They had parked there earlier, way at the back so I wouldn't see the car. And I hadn't. I had no idea they were in the shop with me the whole time. And Sarah was right—let James think that Phillip was raping me.

I went back upstairs. I looked around the shop. It was a mess. An orchestrated mess that would ultimately fool no one. It would simply give me, us, some time. A little breathing space. I walked over to the wall. I looked at myself in the mirror. The one Phillip had said needed re-silvering. I leaned forward and kissed my own image.

—Goodbye, Phillip. It was fun.

I picked up a heavy brass bookend that was at my feet. I stepped back from the wall. Holding the bookend like a hammer, I turned my head away from the mirror and smashed the bookend into it. Without looking back again, I walked over to the front door, my shoes crunching on the broken glass underfoot. I had shut and locked the door while we worked but now I unbolted it, leaving it slightly ajar. I left the burglar alarm switched off.

I went back down through the basement and out the garage doors, closing them for the last time. I climbed into the car, switched on the engine, and looked at the clock. It was exactly midnight.

Jennifer

The plane took off on time at 9:00 o'clock. Midnight in New York. Sandy had driven me to the airport. We avoided the San Diego freeway and took La Cienega all the way. The freeways had become anything but free in Los Angeles and the 405 was the worst of them all. It was the proverbial parking lot. One more car and the whole thing would come to a standstill, never to start again. With no way to get off the exit ramps, people would be living out of their cars. Freeway cities would spring up. Now there's a movie idea.

We pulled up in front of the American Airlines terminal, stopped by a *No Unloading* sign, and got out. A cop was about to move us on when Sandy took me by the waist and kissed me passionately. I kissed back. The cop stared and smiled slyly. Enjoying everything. His wife had better brace herself tonight. He finally walked on, saying nothing. Sandy got my bag from the back seat.

—I hope everything goes all right, she said. —Call me as soon as you see him.

—I will, darling.

I simply squeezed her hand now. We had done our kissing. We had already performed for the benefit of the Los Angeles Police Department. Sandy went around to the driver's side and I headed towards the sliding glass doors of the terminal. I turned back and gave her a final wave.

As I settled into my first class seat, a very handsome steward brought me a glass of Ravenswood Cabernet. If Steven had promised his body to American Airlines, he should start with this nice young man. A small, tight arse squeezed into American Airlines regulation dark blue trousers. A crisp white shirt over a well-sculptured upper-half. Obviously a product of *Gentlemen Gym* on Santa Monica Boulevard. There were still times I thought about men. I loved Sandy. I loved her touch. But there was still this lingering thing—this need for something inside me that was human. The ultimate joining of two bodies. Touching a man's face, feeling his beard. The strength in his arms. I have dreams sometimes that I am having sex with a man. They feel real. Like the drinking dreams that Phillip described to me. Where he really thought he had relapsed. Once, he even went so far as to consider changing his sobriety date. That's how lifelike the dream had been to him.

And then there were the dreams about Gareth still.

My one black experience.

The silky, satiny body. He was lovely. Soft and gentle. Loving my white skin. I remembered stroking down his penis. Sliding one hand over the other to explore his full length and girth. I would lay down, he would stand, and with my head raised off the bed, I could see his cock as he pulled the full length of it out of me before sliding all the way back

in again. Over and over. Perfect rhythm. I shifted in my seat.
—More?

Steward boy was back.

—Yes. Yes, please.

He poured the wine. I looked into his eyes to see if I could engage him. Have his body next to mine a little longer even if it was just while he poured the wine. Whatever his orientation, he was providing service. But he moved on. Back to the galley. And I went back to my thoughts. When I told Phillip about Gareth, he told me about Beverly. She was a beautiful, black woman of around thirty. He showed me a photograph of her. And then he told me all about their sex.

We were on the bed in his house and I had just showered. I was wrapped very loosely in a fluffy towel, leaving lots of skin uncovered and little to the imagination. I was about to moisturize and Phillip said he would do my back for me. He was just wearing his boxer shorts. As we were talking about doing it with Beverly, we both became very horny. But we never crossed that line. All these years, I've wondered though. What it ultimately would have been like. With that deep, deep, shared blood love. With someone you love as much as I loved my brother.

I took one of the Ambien that I kept for Ronnie. I always had them on hand for him. For precisely times like this. For when he had to catch a red-eye somewhere at the last minute. I swallowed it with the last of my wine.

Someone was shaking my shoulder. Steward boy.

—Miss. We're in New York.

Being in first class and being in 2A, I was the second person off the plane. I went straight through baggage claim. Past the row of limo drivers holding up their desperate signs. The signs were almost pleading for me to be the MR. CARLTON or C. WHITMAN they had been designated to pick up. Just as I was thinking I should have organized a limo, that a yellow cab wouldn't take me out to Chester, I saw my name on a Luxury Limos sign: JENNIFER

BROWN, MOTT PRODUCTIONS.

—Someone ordered it for you, I guess, was the driver's response when I asked him how he knew to meet me. I reached for my phone. A text message.

Limo 2 B waiting 4 U. Steven. I texted straight back. THNX.

Good old Steven. Bless him. I went with my new best friend through the exit and out to the street.

It was, as Sandy had promised, wet. Raining like a bastard, as my dad would have said. At that time in the morning, the police let the limos idle by the curb. I hopped into the back of mine.

—I didn't get an address, said the driver. —They said passenger to provide details.

—Well, the details are these. We head up the interstate to Chester and get off at Route 53. Turn right, and I'll direct you from there. I'll know where to go when I see it.

Less than an hour later, we pulled up in front of Phillip's house. It was just getting light. I still had the key he had given me when I was taking care of him after his relapse eleven months ago. I let myself in. The dog started barking.

—Okay, J.C. It's okay.

He needed to pee. I opened the door again and let him out to the garden. The house was cold. Phillip obviously hadn't made a fire last night. It was dark inside despite the breaking dawn. I was suddenly scared, even in these familiar surroundings, and called the dog back in before going any further.

—Come here, J.C. Come with me.

I walked through the dining room and turned on a standing lamp. I fumbled around under the shade of a table lamp in the living room before finally getting it to turn on. I shouted up the stairs.

—Phillip? Phillip?

Nothing.

—Come with me, doggy. We're going upstairs.

Phillip's bedroom door was shut. I gently pushed it

open, calling his name.

His bed hadn't been slept in. It was still meticulously made. When he got sober, he was told to do at least one thing each day that he didn't like doing. As a way of putting discipline back into his life. He hated making beds and so that became his thing.

I went back downstairs. There was a basket on the kitchen counter where Phillip kept his mail and bits and pieces of paper and receipts. He would empty his wallet and pockets each night and anything in there would go into the basket. TBFL he called it. To Be Filed Later. Another name for it was Procrastination with a capital P. No AA discipline here. I quickly flipped through the papers and receipts. Phillip could be sitting on a fortune—there were lottery tickets in here I would gamble more money on that he had never checked.

I looked around the dining room again. I had somehow walked past a beautiful cherry wood box on top of the pine side-table. It was like an over-sized jewelry box. Inlaid. I opened the lid and it revealed a felt-lined partitioned tray. Silver napkin rings filled one of the partitions. An exquisite soup ladle was in another. It seemed to take place of honor, proudly displayed on a square of velvet. There was a tag attached to it. In an elegant script was the identification: *George IV Regency. Rare Irish Soup Ladle. Dublin. 1824. Fiddle pattern.* On the back of the tag was a notation in what seemed to be a woman's handwriting: *You always remember your first!*

—First piece of silver? I wondered. —Or first fuck?

There were two drawers under this top tier with delicate brass handles. I pulled the first drawer open and there was the most beautiful silver cutlery I had ever seen. Forks. Dessert spoons. Teaspoons. Some of them were engraved with what I assumed were family initials. I took one spoon out and looked at the back of it. I knew nothing about silver but from the hallmark and its weight, I knew this must be the real deal. The next drawer down housed a complete collection of silver knives. I slid both drawers back in and went again to the top tier. I picked up one of the napkin rings and examined the tag on that. I held it to the light coming from the standing lamp:

Victorian. Number One of Six. Manchester.

I turned the tag over. No woman's writing this time but a logo: *Remains To Be Seen*. It was set in an elegant typeface with ornate flourishes on the capital letters.

I had just seen that logo! In the basket. I went back over to the kitchen counter and rifled through the papers again. There it was on a sheet of letterhead: *Remains To Be Seen*. There was a second line under the logo: *Antique China and Silver from England*.

The antiques shop! Where Phillip had his love interest. I had asked Phillip if this *Mrs.* was going to leave her *Mr.* for him and he said *that remains to be seen*. The handwriting on this sheet of paper matched that on the soup ladle tag. I read the short note very carefully. It was dated March 27th. An instruction to meet.

1:30 tomorrow. *Bistro Bijoux*. We have to talk.

No signature. No name. Obviously meant for Phillip though. Why would he have it otherwise? It hardly took Sherlock Holmes to figure out that the mystery *Mrs.* of the antiques shop needed to talk to Phillip over lunch. And it sounded serious.

The letterhead told me *Remains To Be Seen* was at *12 Spring Lane, Old Woodford*. That was only twenty minutes away.

I had a hunch. It sounded like *Bistro Bijoux* was a regular meeting place. It was very pointed in the note. Not: Let's meet at *Bistro Bijoux* for a change. Or: How about *Bistro Bijoux*? It was: *Bistro Bijoux*. Period. Where we always meet. That's what lovers did. They found a place where they knew they would be safe. Or where they could explain themselves if someone saw them. Knowing the generosity of my brother, he would probably be paying for these meals with the Mrs. I dug through the basket again. Bingo.

A restaurant receipt. *Bistro Bijoux*. Old Woodford. Two

people. A glass of wine and a Perrier with cranberry juice. That would be Phillip's. He called it his AA cocktail. This receipt was from the 26th. They had lunch. I turned the receipt over. Phillip had written on it as if keeping a record of what the lunch was for: 'S' leaving 'J'.

I went back outside. The limo was still there. The driver was asleep in the front seat. The seat was pushed all the way back. He was obviously hiding from work. Taking a nap before the next job. In Phillip's fucking driveway! I smiled for the first time since I had left Sandy. What a bloody cheek. Only in New York, as they say.

I opened the garage, but there was no car. I knew Phillip had an Audi Estate. He bought it as much for the dog as himself. J.C. had his own bed in the back.

Okay, Agatha Christie. Let's recap. They had lunch on the 26th. She leaves him a note on the 27th. She wants lunch again the next day, the 28th. That was yesterday. Phillip didn't sleep in the house last night. He probably hadn't been here since late yesterday morning. I spoke to him just before noon New York time. Told him all about Sandy. The dog obviously hadn't been out in a while. His legs were crossed when I came in and then he peed for an eternity out in the garden. Phillip had obviously taken his car. He said he was going to try to catch an AA meeting before an appointment he was anxious to keep. If he kept his appointment, it was the lunch at *Bistro Bijoux* yesterday. The restaurant wouldn't be open right now obviously and an antiques shop probably wouldn't open until eleven at the earliest. As much as I wanted to go straight down there, it wouldn't do much good. I wouldn't be able to find out anything. I'd go back in, have some tea, and then find a way down to Old Woodford a little later. Suddenly the limo door opened. My trusty driver had woken up.

—Can I use the bathroom?

—Why not take a shower while you're at it? You've already had a good kip in the driveway. How about some pancakes?

He looked at me, totally uncomprehending.

–Sorry?

–Doesn't matter.

I walked back into the house and he followed me.

–First door on the left.

He disappeared into the loo and I put the kettle on. Then a thought occurred to me. Of course. I could go down to Old Woodford now—I'd be early but I had a ride. I turned off the kettle. I could get a tea or coffee in the village.

When the driver reappeared, I stopped him before he could leave.

–Are you going back out to JFK?

–No, I'm going to Manhattan. I have a pick-up at nine. That's why I was taking a nap. Killing time.

I looked at the kitchen clock. It was still only seven forty-five.

–I'm coming with you, I said. –I'm going somewhere that's on the way.

The dog sensed we were on the move and went nuts at the thought he was being left alone again.

–You can come too, I told J.C.

–Not in my car, Missy.

–Listen mate. I happen to know you just took a shit in my brother's bathroom. Which, quite frankly, is taking a fucking liberty if you ask me. So you owe me. The dog is coming with us. And don't call me Missy.

We all climbed into the car. I surprised myself by remembering the back roads to Old Woodford, through Walton Ridge. And it was closer than I had thought. We pulled in the village a few minutes after eight. There were very few cars or people about. As if by divine intervention, I caught sight of *Bistro Bijoux* out of the corner of my eye. And there was the Audi. Phillip's car was looking sad and lonely in the rain, just as the last car left in a parking lot always does.

–Drive me around to that car. Drop me right next to it so I don't get wet.

As the limo pulled up to the Audi, I lowered my window to see better. The raindrops on the glass were obscuring my view. From this angle and distance, I could see something under the car. As we got closer, I saw what it was: a bunch of keys were on the ground by the driver's door. If you were standing next to the car, you would never have seen them. I looked over at the entrance to the restaurant and noted there was a separate door to the bar. It didn't take much to figure this one out. Phillip had his lunch date. They might both have gone into the bar afterwards. Or he went alone. He started drinking again. He got drunk. He came out. Dropped his car keys before opening the car door. So drunk, he didn't realize and left them on the ground. Then he wandered off somewhere.

The dog was barking now. He recognized the car.

–Okay, thanks. We'll get out. Goodbye. I was only pretending to be mad about you taking a shit. You're welcome anytime.

The driver shook his head and drove off. I picked up the keys from under the car and pressed the unlock symbol on the fob. A click all round. I went to the back of the car and lifted up the tailgate. J.C. hopped in.

I adjusted the driver's seat. We might have been twins but Phillip had at least three inches over me. I couldn't quite reach the pedals from his driving position.

I started the car and finally figured out the windshield wipers. It would be much better if they were the same on every car. When I rule the world, I'll insist on that. I pulled forward and swung in a long arc around the empty lot and out to the road. It was a small village. If my memory served me well, Spring Lane would be very close. I think next to the old movie house.

I drove slowly, not realizing I was following the exact path Phillip had taken. Past the firehouse. Past the historical society. Past the church. *Bingo* again. Spring Lane. The rain was really coming down now and it was hard to see anything. The shop was suddenly right in front of me.

I saw the parking spaces first. *Reserved for Remains To Be Seen.* I pulled in and looked back at the dog.

–You stay here, buster. I'll be back in a second.

The moment I opened the car door, the rain hit me. I stood up and braced myself against it. Despite my raincoat I was clearly going to get soaked.

I took the steps to the front door as fast as I could without slipping. I had to strain to see against the rain and it was only at the last moment that I realized the door to the shop was actually a few inches ajar. Like the keys under the car, it was something you could have easily missed.

I hesitated. This didn't feel right. Keys on the ground by Phillip's car. And just a quarter of a mile away, his lover's shop door left open. I should phone the police. No. Go in. Look first.

I pushed the door open. There was still very little daylight because of the heavy rainclouds. The shop was in semidarkness. I stepped in. There was an immediate crunching under my feet. Glass. I squinted against the darkness to get a better look at what I was standing on. Glass and broken china.

The shop was disaster. There had been rummaging everywhere. Pictures were obviously missing from the walls—all that remained were hooks and patches of darker wallpaper that, hidden behind the pictures, hadn't faded evenly with the exposed areas.

Something was wrong. This was too orchestrated. An arranged robbery.

My film production experience kicked in. This is how a typical over the top Hollywood film art director might make a robbery look. He'd try to make it authentic by using his arms to sweep things from their safe places and make them crash to the floor for maximum effect. Turning a table upside down. The safe broken open. And then the director would come in and tone it down a bit. Less mess, he would say, it's all a bit clichéd. And then the stagehands would move some of the broken bits and pieces and the less is more moment would reign. Would a robber really leave the front door open? In the movies, maybe.

I had no doubt this had all been staged. My intuition was hard at work. But that still didn't answer the fucking question. Where was Phillip? I looked for clues among the mess. Nothing. I found my way down to the basement. Nothing. Back in the shop, I went over to a wall where a gilt edged mirror was still hanging. It had been smashed leaving jagged shards of glass clinging precariously to the edge of the frame. I took it down carefully. My film sensibilities wanted there to be another safe behind here. A hidden one. But there was just the bare wall.

I could hear water dripping. I put my ear against the wall. There must be a chimney or something in there. Maybe a fireplace that had been blocked up and now the heavy rain had found its way in.

I could also hear the dog barking. He probably needed to go potty again. I crunched my way back out of the shop and down to the car. From this angle, I had a clear view of the roof. I looked for a chimney. But there was nothing. The dog was going crazy.

I opened the tailgate to let him out and suddenly realized I didn't have a leash. He had hopped into the limo at Phillip's. Hopped out and into the Audi at the restaurant. And now he was out of the car and spinning around in circles. Phillip had told me about this—when he wanted pee-pee, when he wanted feeding. Suddenly J.C. bounded up the steps and ran towards the shop. I chased after him. I didn't want him cutting his paws on the glass but he was already in the shop before I could grab his collar. He was standing at the wall where the gilt mirror had hung. Barking at it. His tail wagging furiously.

—What, is it?

And then I remembered.

I had asked Phillip what he would do if his love interest's husband stopped by and caught him in the shop. Hop in the closet? Ha! Ha! he had laughed. Something like that, he said.

More of a cupboard. A hidden cupboard. One her husband didn't know about.

I stood in front of the blank wall. There was still the sound of water dripping. I tapped the wall. The dog barked.

–Shhh. Listen.

I banged again. It seemed solid. I moved over a bit and banged again. It was like looking for a stud to hang a picture. You wanted the solid sound, not the empty one. I got the empty one. The wall echoed. And so did Phillip's voice in my head: *J.C. seems to know where I am at all times.* Now the dog was spinning around furiously. I banged again. The wall suddenly swung wide open. A hidden door. I lost my footing as I stumbled back. J.C. cowered.

A garbage bag, six-foot high tumbled out of the inner space. Like a broom that hadn't been put away in the cupboard properly. Or a giant jack-in-the box springing free from its captivity. It scared the shit out of me. It tumbled and crashed to the ground with a thud just as I rolled out of its way. I lay on the ground among the broken china and glass staring at it.

–Oh, my god. Oh, my god.

I knew that thud. It was the sound film stunt men made when they were faking death, after supposedly being shot, or whacked over the head. Hitting the ground like a dead weight.

And I knew that shape. The bag held a body.

Phillip's. Fuck.

Epilogue

The Irish Countryside, Twenty miles west of Dublin.

After the *rape* as Susan also now called it, she and James returned to their country home outside Dublin. It was a limestone mansion, built around 1815 during the English military occupation of Ireland. It had been built for one Major General Lionel Birley, an officer in the *Dubs*, the nickname for The Royal Dublin Fusiliers.

Successive generations of Birley's had served in the Dubs and the home remained in the family. A perfect museum and showcase for Susan's collection of Georgian silver and antiques.

They had pretty much cleaned out the shop after wrapping Phillip in plastic garbage bags and dumping him unceremoniously in the *Ha-Ha* cupboard.

They had anticipated the police would eventually find him. But the *Ha-Ha* cupboard's secret was discovered by Jennifer who came looking for her brother the very next day. She obviously had remarkable instincts for tracking down her twin.

The New York police now wanted to talk to James and Susan, of course. Their mysterious disappearance. The botched attempt at giving the impression of a robbery.

For the time being though, they were safe.

Despite warm political relations between Washington and Dublin, it has always been notoriously difficult for the US to bring suspects and escaped felons back from the Republic of Ireland. Cases going as far back as 1904 are still cited. No one had been extradited to the US for years. Including murder suspects. Even if the process were to be started, James and Susan would probably be long gone to that permanent safe haven in the sky before the order came down.

But should they be extradited, the line of defense would be convincing. James sincerely believed Phillip was raping Susan. And Susan encouraged this more and more as the days and weeks passed. A high-powered lawyer would contend that James simply attacked the attacker. They panicked and fled because of what they had done. The lawyer would tell the court their only crime was to flee a society where the word *rape* had become synonymous with *personal moral failure*. Where the term *victim* had become a pejorative—as America's liberal media were quick to point out.

Sarah's motivation for the blow she delivered wasn't about rape. The blow might not even have been meant for Phillip. But her ability to forgive Susan was greater than her anger and she remained at her side. She had taken care of all the details. She had long ago promised that she would do anything for Susan and she proved that out. They worked through the night packing up the paintings and silver. Susan made a crack of dawn call to the prudent shipper who often spirited valuables in and out of the country for her wealthiest clients. The shipper knew not to ask any questions.

They were all on separate flights to Ireland and England before anyone knew they had left.

James into Shannon, Susan directly to Dublin, and Sarah into Manchester before going by rail to Liverpool and taking the ferry over to Belfast. She travelled down by road from there.

Sarah's role in the household was a little ambiguous. Old friend? Guest? Servant?

It didn't matter to Sarah. All that mattered was that Susan was safe. And that she, Sarah, was close to her. James was safe too and Susan was happy to be close to him.

Sarah served dinner on the Denby platter in the formal dining room.

Irish lamb, new potatoes with mint from the kitchen garden, and asparagus from the ancient beds that generations of Birley's had cultivated and dined on.

James wandered in from the library, carrying his evening Irish malt.

Susan was beautiful in a black wool dress that was neither formal nor casual but simply, Susan.

They sat down. James poured red wine for the ladies. Sarah got back up to dim the chandelier. Susan lighted the candles.

They burned fiercely in a pair of Georgian silver candlesticks.

Postscript

Phillip

I remembered having lunch with Susan. She told me she had to go away for a little while but that she'd be back. And that's all I can remember about that day.

After that, it's a complete blackout. Blackouts are scary. I woke up in hospital.

Jen told me there had been a robbery at *Remains To Be Seen*.

That I must have gone there and disturbed the thieves. I had been hit twice over the head with something that had a sharp edge. They thought both times with the same instrument.

I was apparently left unconscious in a locked closet. That would be the *Ha-Ha* cupboard. Which was strange, because I thought only Susan and Sarah knew about it.

I was in hospital for more than three weeks.

The wounds had punctured the base of my skull. Just missing the vertebrae connecting my head to my spine.

I should have died.

Like I should have died after the seizures brought on by my alcoholism.

My out-of-control drinking.

I had been spared. I had been given the precious gift of life for a second time. The gift that keeps on giving. And both times, my beautiful darling sister saved me.

I get headaches. Sharp pains in the back of my head. Jen

199

said she knew exactly how they felt.

When I came out of hospital, I had to go back to Four Oaks Rehab. The same place I was admitted after my big drunk.

The injuries close to my spine had affected my motor skills.

Gradually though, the feeling came back into my legs.

I was in physical therapy every day for more than a month. I still have to go once a week.

I will never walk properly again. I walk with the help of a cane.

There's something in the way he moves.

Slowly and with a limp. That's how I move now.

Jennifer stayed the whole time. Serendipity played a role here.

Paramount Pictures decided that Ronnie's new film would be better shot on a New York stage. Using New England locations.

This made everyone happy. Everyone except Sandy. She stayed behind in L.A. and flew out when she could to see Jen. Theirs became a bi-coastal relationship. And in Jen's case, I think a bi-sexual one. I think she was shagging a bloke on the crew as well. I love my sister.

I naturally asked her for all the details about what had happened at *Remains To Be Seen* that day, but all she ever told me was this:

–If dogs have a heaven, Phillip, then J.C. will have a wonderful home.

I knew she was holding things back. And I also knew that one day, she would tell me what.

–When you're better, she had said.

I do have one other vague memory. Total blackness. I heard and felt water dripping on me but I wasn't getting wet. It was like one of my alcoholic hallucinations.

There was the sound of water on plastic. And then a dog barking. I remember struggling to my feet. Leaning against something solid and falling down flat.

Nothing else.

I have trouble sleeping. I dream about Susan a lot.

I went back to the shop but it was empty. A realtor's sign outside.

I couldn't understand this. Susan said she was coming back. Why would she sell the shop?

Maybe she didn't want to live with the ghosts of the robbery. To work at the scene of the crime, as it were.

I went to Susan's house.

I knew I shouldn't have.

Off-limits. Out of bounds. Forbidden Territory. Danger. Do not enter.

But I couldn't stay away. I had to see her, find out where Susan was.

But the house was empty. Boarded up. No Susan. No James. No Sarah. Yellow *Do Not Cross* tape at the end of the driveway keeping nosey parkers like me at bay.

I kept asking Jen about it and she finally told me a totally ridiculous story.

The police thought Susan and James, and maybe even Sarah, had faked the robbery. And that I had walked in on them. That they had caused my injuries.

I started laughing.

—Why on earth would Susan do that, Jen? Susan loved me. She loved my body. She wouldn't hurt me. And anyway, Susan is going to leave James. She wants to be with me. She had said she never wanted it to end between us. And it won't. She told me that she simply needed to do it in her own way. She told me that. She's just had to go away for a little while to sort it all out, then she'll be back. And we'll be together. Just like the poem I wrote for her.

I closed my eyes and recited it for Jen.

Separate lives
In the same little town.
When you were up,
I might have been down.

Parallel paths
No encounter we had.
When I was happy,
You might have been sad.
Living apart
So near yet so far.
Did we look up
And gaze the same star?
Then under one roof
The look that said—Yes!
We fell madly in love,
Nothing more, nothing less.
Our eyes, then our hearts,
Our bodies we tethered.
Together at last,
And at last, we're together.

I opened my eyes when I had finished, expecting Jen to say something like: Oh, that's beautiful, Phillip.

But she just looked sad.

I couldn't understand it, I was happy. Things always work out. I had total faith in that. Susan was coming back.

Jennifer started stroking my head.

—When? she asked.

Big tears rolled down her cheeks. I leaned over and tried to wipe them but she brushed my hand away. She was upset. More upset than I had ever seen her.

—When, Phillip? When is Susan coming back? When exactly do you think you're going to be together? Oh, Phillip!

Jennifer was crying and shaking her head. I took my darling sister in my arms and stroked her hair. She didn't understand. I didn't know the answers.

And it didn't matter.

—I don't know, Jennifer. All that remains to be seen. But Susan will be back. She said she would.

About Words In The Works

Words In The Works bridges the gap between traditional publishers and self-publishing helping new and established authors enjoy all the benefits of the self-publishing process without having to learn it themselves. We are specialists in Kindle Direct Publishing (KDP) for Amazon and offer print and eBook formatting, cover design, editing, and ghostwriting services.

Write: info@wordsintheworks.com

Or visit: www.wordsintheworks.com

Made in the USA
Columbia, SC
14 September 2019